# THE DAY TO REMEMBER

*Emma's Series - Book Two*

*What happens when the dream is over
and reality sets in?*

JESSICA WOOD

This book is a work of fiction. Names, characters, places, and incidents either are the product of the author's imagination or are used fictitiously. Any resemblance to actual persons, living or dead, events, or locales is entirely coincidental.

Copyright © 2013 by Jessica Wood

All rights reserved. Except as permitted under the U.S. Copyright Act of 1976, no part of this book may be reproduced, scanned, distributed, or transmitted in any form or by any means, or stored in a database or retrieval system, without the prior written permission of the author.

ISBN-13: 978-1492286295

ISBN-10: 149228629X

eBook ISBN-13 978-1-940285-01-6

First Edition: August 2013

## Acknowledgements

There are many people that deserve my sincere gratitude. This book would not have been possible without your part in it.

To my family—my lifeline, thank you for not only tolerating my often-crazy ideas, but embracing them with me and allowing me to be who I am as I started this journey towards something I truly love. Your constant support—both spoken and unspoken—means more than you can imagine.

I want to also thank everyone who read and loved *A Night to Forget*. Thank you for taking a chance on a brand new author. It was your interest and support that encouraged me to continue writing, and for that, I'm forever grateful.

A special thanks to J.S. Cooper for being my writing buddy from afar. I'm really excited for us to finally be living in the same city again!

A big thanks to my beta readers for reading this book while it was being drafted. Thank you for putting your valuable time and effort into this book, and into me. This was especially true for the following people: Dawn Collins, Maria D., Angie Durnin, Katrina Evans, Marci Flores, Gillian Hedges, Gloria Herrera, Madelyn Medina-Nunez, Diane Robson, Kathy Shreve, Tanya Skaggs, Sweetdee, and Carrie White. Thank you for clearing your schedule to read my last draft the second you received it. I appreciate your time more than you will know.

Thanks to my amazing street team for all that you do. You guys are the best! I cannot thank you enough for all of your support and encouragement from the very beginning of my crazy journey as an author.

# The Day to Remember

*To everyone who believes that in dreams and in love, there are no impossibilities.*

# PROLOGUE

*"If you press me to say why I loved him,
I can say no more than because he was he,
and I was I."* – Michel de Montaigne

*Emma*

I found myself standing in the middle of a large, dark clearing surrounded by trees. A brilliant, icy-blue, full moon casted its gentle light down from above. A cool breeze blew through my hair, bringing the sounds of a melody to my ears. I looked around the clearing, searching for the source of the soothing tune.

I found it. From about a hundred yards away, soft lights illuminated from the edge of the forest where the trees were sparse. From where I stood, the lights were like twinkling stars suspended around the trees. There, I saw someone—a man—standing among those trees. Instinctually, I moved towards him. The thick grass was lush and damp under my feet at every step. Then, as if sensing my approach, the man looked up and saw me. He smiled, and I froze at the sight of his deep-set dimples—the same dimples that had once melted my heart. It was *him*.

My heart raced and I was consumed with an irresistible urge to run from this clearing—to run away from this man. But my body would not listen. Instead, I felt myself walking across the clearing, closing the distance between us. As I came closer towards him, I saw thousands of small lights wrapped around the trees and thousands more dangled down in long, thin strands like falling stars. Brandon stood in the middle of these lights, playing a guitar. His fingers melodically strummed Elvis Presley's "I Can't Help Falling in Love with You." His eyes were full of emotion as he watched me approach him. By the time I was standing in front of him, my eyes were filled with tears that were threatening their way down my face.

At the end of the song, he placed the guitar on the grass and he reached for my hands. "Hi. You came." He gave me another smile. "I want to be that fool that rushes in with you, because I can't help falling in love with you," he said sincerely as he echoed the lyrics of the song.

I looked at him and felt my heart ache with happiness and sorrow. I blinked and hot tears streamed down my cheeks. "But … but what about her?" The image of the other girl—the stunning girl I saw at the door the other morning—was all I could think about when I looked at Brandon.

He smiled at me as he held my face with his hands and gently whipped away my tears. "She means nothing to me. *You* are the one that I want to be with. You are the world I want be in. Forever and always."

Our eyes met and I felt my anger towards him waver at his words. "I am?"

"You are."

"But—but why was she there?"

"I don't know." His face was full of regret. "She shouldn't have been there. I'm really sorry you had to meet her."

I looked at him in confusion. His brown eyes were gentle and sincere, and I knew I believed him. No matter how much pain he had caused me, for some inextricable reason, I believed him. "You broke my heart, Brandon," I said softly. I looked down to avoid his gaze. I could not bear for him to see the pain that was undoubtedly reflected in my eyes.

"I know, and I'm so sorry. Please believe me when I say I would never intentionally hurt you."

His hands were warm against my face and his thumbs gently stroked my cheeks. I closed my eyes and allowed my face to sink into his touch—to feel the familiar roughness of his hands against my skin. "I want to believe you," I whispered. I felt torn between what my heart and what my head was telling me.

He pulled me into his warm embrace and I buried my face into the contours of his hard chest and inhaled his scent. He gently kissed my head and whispered back, "Tell me what I need to do for you to believe me."

I sighed against the heat of his body. Being with him, in his embrace, was home to me. It felt right and I knew there was nowhere else I wanted to be but here. "Just don't leave me.

Don't let me go." I pressed myself against him and felt his arms tighten around me.

"I won't. And I don't ever want to."

I moved my face up to look at him. He looked down at me and I saw the love in his eyes—the same love that I felt in my heart for him. Our lips met in a deep all-consuming kiss, and all my worries melted away like ice cubes in the heat of his touch. My lips eagerly explored his—soft and salty. Our tongues found one another, moving in unison, swirling and sucking. His hands moved down the small of my back and he pulled me closer against his body, pressing his manhood against my lower stomach. I gasped in surprised by how hard his erection had grown against me.

"Can you feel how much my body responds to you?" His voice was ragged and I heard the need in his voice.

I nodded and gasped again, "As much as my body wants you." I rubbed myself against him, hungry for his touch and desperate for him to be connected to me.

Then, suddenly, something from the corner of my eyes caught my attention. Just a few feet away from us stood a full-length mirror in a gold, ornate frame. *Was that there earlier?* I pulled away from Brandon's embrace and looked up at him, frowning in confusion. "What's that doing here?"

He didn't seem to hear my question and pulled me towards him again, kissing my neck as his hands explored my back. I moaned in pleasure, and tried to push my curiosity for the mirror out of my mind.

But I couldn't. Something compelled me towards the mirror and I found myself moving away from Brandon's embrace and towards it. I walked the few feet in the direction of the mirror, holding Brandon's hand and leading him with me.

When I positioned myself in front of the mirror, I gasped in shock at its reflection and dropped Brandon's hand. There in the mirror, staring back at me, was *her*—the stunning brunette I saw at the door that morning, the one that had looked at me with disgust, the one whose words shattered my hopes of happiness with Brandon—his *girlfriend*. But, she wasn't next to me and she wasn't behind me. She *was* me. I was her and she was me.

My eyes flew open and I sat straight up in bed. My body was covered in cold sweat. My heart was pounding violently against my chest as I tried to catch my breath and shake off the images I just saw from my mind. That was another dream—no, not a dream, a nightmare. Brandon had professed his love to *her*. He desired *her*. *She* was his world. Not me.

# CHAPTER ONE
## *Emma*

It was 6:35 a.m. and I was wide awake. I have not been able to fall back to sleep since the dream three hours ago. It was Tuesday morning, and it had been two days, 21 hours, and 15 minutes since I last saw Brandon and two days, 10 hours, and 40 minutes since I spoke to him. Yet, for the last three days, he had plagued every second of my thoughts since that heart-wrenching moment Saturday morning when I came face to face with Brandon's girlfriend. The words, "Brandon's girlfriend"—a title that had so recently belonged to me—now felt like a sharp, cold dagger to my heart. A wave of excruciating pain washed through me and my heart tightened at the thought of Brandon with someone else.

Despite my best efforts, I was again pulled back to the memories of that morning. Brandon and I had just made love for the second time and I had never felt as happy as I had that morning in his arms. I thought I had finally found the man that had made me feel whole, alive, and loved. But that happiness was as fleeting as an elusive dream, and within minutes, my world had tumbled down like a stack of playing cards built on lies.

When I saw the shock, recognition, and guilt in Brandon's eyes at the sight of the gorgeous brunette at the door, I just knew that she must have been telling the truth and that she meant something important to him.

Everything after that point was a blur. I remembered grabbing my purse at the end table next to the door and immediately running past the brunette and out of his condo without looking back. I must have been in hysterics when I rushed out because I have flashbacks of me hyperventilating as I huddled in the corner of the elevator floor as it took me down to the lobby. At some point, I must have gotten up from the floor, left Brandon's building, and found my way back home, because there I was, standing in the doorway of my studio apartment with no idea of how I got home.

My body trembled, yet I knew it wasn't cold. I was in a daze, as if in a foggy dream with no understanding of where I was, how I got there, or even who I was. My body felt numb as disbelief seemed to encapsulate me in a cocoon that temporarily sheltered me from the pain that would eventually come.

And come it did.

In a brief moment of clarity, I looked down and realized I ran out of Brandon's place without changing into my clothes—I was still in his button-up shirt and boxers. In a crazed frenzy, I ripped off his clothes from my body, as if they were on fire and searing my skin.

But at the sight of his clothes in a lifeless heap on my living room floor, I began to cry. No, I did not just cry, I broke down. I collapsed next to that heap and sobbed so violently, my naked body shook with devastating abandonment. *How did everything go so wrong?* I thought.

After what must have been an hour or two, I pulled myself up from the floor and grabbed my phone out of my purse so I could call the girls. I noticed that I had four missed calls and two voicemails from Brandon. Unable to resist hearing his voice and hearing what he had to say, I listened to his voicemails.

I clicked on the first voicemail and put the phone to my ear. "Emma? What the hell, Emma, please pick up. Why did you leave like that? Please call me back."

I blinked back the tears and clicked on the next message. "Emma, I've been trying to get Des—I mean, Desiree—to tell me what exactly she said to you, but she said she didn't say anything to you. But why did you run out? What happened? Can you just call me?"

The stunning brunette had a name. Desiree. There was a familiarity in his voice when he said her name, as if he'd said her name many times before. I felt devastated and defeated. Part of me wanted to confront him, to hit him, and to make him feel the unbearable pain that weighed on my heart. Another part of me could not imagine facing him, and feared that seeing him or talking to him would cause further pain that my heart could not withstand.

I couldn't talk to him right now. I didn't want to face the reality of Brandon's relationship with Desiree. Instead of calling him back, I sent a text to Jill, Steph, and Gloria: *He has a girlfriend! A fucking girlfriend! I think I'm still in shock. Last night was perfect with him. How did it all turn out so horribly wrong so quickly??? I'm a mess and need to be alone right now. I'm not ready to talk about it, but needed to tell you guys. Love you guys and miss you!*

I quickly turned off my phone. My head was spinning, struggling between who I thought Brandon was and who he really was—who he was with Desiree. I crawled the few feet to my bed and allowed my body to sink under the protective layers of my sheets and comforter, away from the external world, away from reality, and away from Brandon. I laid there in silence, and in a state of paralysis. My eyes were opened, yet I saw nothing. I felt myself slip in and out of consciousness as I replayed over and over again what had happened.

I must have fallen asleep at some point because when I opened my eyes, soft, melancholy hues of pink and orange painted the sky outside my window. *It must have been early evening*, I thought. I closed my eyes, willing myself to return to my dreamless sleep, to return to the void where there were no thoughts and there were no pain. But sleep didn't come, and thoughts of Brandon trickled into my consciousness and the too-familiar numbing ache began to wrap itself around my battered heart.

I let out a deep sigh, trying to ignore the feelings that consumed my body. I slowly reached for my phone to turn it on. It was 7:45 p.m. *Had I really been in bed for the last eight hours?*

I saw several text messages and voicemails from the girls. There was also a text from Brandon. I felt my body tighten with anxiety as I clicked through the messages.

Jill: *OMG!*

Steph: *WTF! A girlfriend? What's his number?*

Jill: *Are you okay??? I just tried calling you, but it's going straight to voicemail. Call me please! I'm here to listen when you're ready! Xoxo!!!*

Steph: *No better yet, what's the bitch's number? I want to give both of them a piece of my mind!*

Gloria: *No way! What the hell! Are you sure? You okay?*

Steph: *Are you okay? Got your voicemail! Call me! Love you!*

Gloria: *What happened?? Call me if you need to talk? <3*

Steph: *Fuck him! You deserve better than a cheating shithead!*

Brandon: *Emma, what the hell is going on? Please call me.*

Just then, I heard the intercom to my door buzz. I ignored it. I was about to turn off my phone and force myself back to sleep when my phone beeped. Another text. I looked at the screen and felt another wave of anxiety ripple through me. It was another text from Brandon: *I'm outside your building. Please buzz me in. Stop ignoring me, we need to talk.*

My body froze. He was downstairs. It was him that had buzzed my intercom a moment ago. As if to confirm my thoughts, the intercom buzzed again. Anxiety prickled down my body. I wasn't ready to see him. I wasn't ready to hear what he had to say. I wasn't ready for him to break my heart all over again.

Then another text came through my phone. *I know you're probably home, Emma, and I'm not leaving until you talk to me. And if you're not home, I'm going to wait out here until you come home. Please talk to me.*

I felt panic course through me at his words. Before I could talk myself out of it, I forced myself to call him. He picked up at the first ring.

"Emma? Where the hell are you? Are you home?" I heard Brandon say in a rushed voice on the other end of the line.

"Brandon, I need to be alone right now, I—" I stopped mid-sentence. There were so many things I wanted to say to him and to ask him, but at that moment, I was unsure of what to say—what I was ready to say to him. I felt a mixture of hurt, anger, and love towards him, and I knew I wasn't ready to confront him—not when I felt this vulnerable.

"Emma, why did you leave so abruptly this morning? What the hell happened?"

"Are you serious?" I heard myself ask with an air of defiance that surprised me. "How could you have not told me? You made a fool out of me, Brandon. You asked me to go get the door because you expected the courier, but I see *her* standing there! Did you honestly expect me to stick around and hang out with you two?" I spat out the words and felt a wave of anger come over me.

There was silence on the other line, which both made me nervous and increased my anger. "Emma, I'm not sure what to say. I didn't mean to upset you. I didn't know Des was—"

"Do *not* say her name to me! How could you, Brandon?" I felt hot angry tears well up in my eyes.

"Emma, I'm not trying to upset you, but I think you're overreacting. She's—"

"Overreacting? How can you say that? How could you have slept with me and not told me about her?" I asked accusatorially.

"Emma, stop being this way. It's not a big deal. I had a life before I met you, just like you had one before you met me."

"So you don't deny it then?" My voice was scathing.

"Deny what? What the hell am I suppose to deny here?" I could hear the irritation in Brandon's voice and I flinched at his reproach.

"Deny that—" I paused and felt my streak of heated boldness waver. "—that you didn't tell me about her."

I heard Brandon sigh into the phone with frustration. "Please be reasonable here. Emma, I don't think I need to tell you everything about my life. We haven't known each other for that long, and my relationship with Des isn't something I really want to have a conversation with you about."

His last few words ignited the anger that I could no longer suppress. "Yes, Brandon, you're so fucking right. We haven't known each other for that long, so of course I wouldn't think to ask you if you have any other relationships. I thought you were this sweet guy who actually cared about me. I thought you were falling in love with me! And you're right, you don't *need* to tell me everything about your life, but I thought you would *want* to because you wanted me to be a part of it. And I'd think with something so important as your relationship with that other girl, you'd think it'd be important to tell me. How incredibly stupid of me, right? Why on earth would you want more from me than my virginity and another notch on your belt?"

"Emma, that's really out of line. You know I want more from you than that." I could hear the anger in his voice, which seemed to further fuel my anger.

I ignored his comment. "You know what? I really feel sorry for her! You may have made a fool out of me, but you've made a bigger fool out of her and the relationship you have with her. I hope you have a great fucking life with your girlfriend. Don't call me again."

"What the fuck, Emma, Des is—" I heard Brandon say before I ended the call. I took a deep, ragged breath and wiped the remaining tears from my face. *I will NOT cry over this man. He does NOT deserve my tears.* I told me myself with conviction—a conviction that was absent from my heart. My phone buzzed, causing me to jump. Brandon's name popped up on the screen and I immediately pressed "Ignore" before I could change my mind. Then it buzzed again. A text from him. I deleted it without reading its contents. The intercom buzzed again. I put my hands to my ears and shook my head, willing him to go away. I didn't think my heart could bear any more pain from this man.

I quickly pulled up Jill's number on my phone to call her. I felt panicked and needed to talk to someone—someone that wasn't Brandon.

"Sweetie? I'm glad you called. Are you okay? What happened? Tell me everything—if you're up to it, that is." Jill's concerned voice came rushing through the phone.

"I'm not sure. I don't know how I'm feeling right now. I think I'm still in shock. I just talked to him on the phone and I screamed and cursed at him. That's so unlike me, but I just couldn't hold it in. I was so upset."

"What? You just talked to him? What happened? Can we start from the beginning?"

I took a deep, tired breath, "Okay. Sorry, I know I sound like a mess. God, it's been awful, Jill. Where do I even begin?"

"It's okay. You're not a mess. You just sound like you went through something awful, and that's totally okay. Just remember, you'll be alright. No matter what happened, you *will* be okay." Jill's reassuring voice was soothing and I realized how much I've missed her—the sister I never had, but a sister nonetheless. "So maybe we can start from the top. We briefly talked yesterday morning before work and you said you were heading over to Brandon's place because he had a special night planned for you two. What ended up happening?"

I took a deep breath to calm myself. "Well, we had an amazing night last night. I mean, everything was just perfect." I buried my face in my free hand that wasn't holding the phone. "I—I just don't know how everything got to this point." Tears once again filled my eyes. I told Jill in excruciating detail about the canopy bed and candles Brandon had set up outside his terrace that overlooked the sunset. "He was my first, Jill. And … and it was amazing. At that moment, I really thought he was the one."

"Oh sweetie," Jill crooned sympathetically.

"Jill, I know this is going to sound silly, but there was a moment when he was on top of me and looking into my eyes, and I felt the world actually standing still. It was like I could sense the magic in that moment and everything slowed down for it. It was nothing I've ever felt before."

"Oh hun, that's not silly. I've never felt that before with anyone, but it sounds wonderful. That's how my mom described how she felt towards my dad when he proposed. She said it felt like magic, like the world stopped for that brief moment to celebrate that perfect moment between them." Jill paused for a second before continuing, "So, what happened then? I mean, it sounds like a perfect night."

I told Jill about the girl at the door, about what she said, about the guilty look on Brandon's face and the panic in his eyes, and about the conversation I just had with Brandon moments earlier.

"Wow, I'm so sorry, Emma. How could he do this?" Jill paused while I began to sob quietly. "Emma … are you sure? I know I've never met him, but from everything you've told me about him, he just doesn't seem like the type that'd do this."

"I really don't want to believe it, but she obviously knew him well. She knew where he lives, she knew his name, she knew I was wearing his shirt, and she felt comfortable enough showing up randomly on a Saturday morning. Plus, why would she say she's a guy's girlfriend to another girl when she's not, especially when the other girl is half-naked in the guy's clothes opening the door to the guy's house?"

"God, why would he do this? I just don't get men. He sounded like he was so sweet and genuine, and he seemed to really adore you."

"I thought he did too, but maybe I was lying to myself. Maybe I saw what I wanted to see, and not what was really there." I sighed and felt the heaviness of my heart. The images I had of my life with Brandon earlier this morning were gone, as if those images were made from a canvas of colored dust and a violent gust of wind just blew it apart and into nothing.

"Is there anything you want me to do? Gloria and Steph are both back in California in two weeks for Thanksgiving. We can all drive to San Francisco on Friday and see you.

"You mean *Black* Friday," I said with the wry laugh.

"Oh Emma, don't think about it too much, or it'll just eat at you. Maybe he just wasn't the right guy for you. My dad always said that the right guy will fight for you and your love at all costs and despite the obstacles."

"I love your dad. He's such a sweet man." I thought about Jill's father and how he uprooted his life and moved from London to California for Jill's mother after only a few months together. He had already known that she was the one and he had done everything in his power to make their relationship work. My heart ached at that thought—not just for myself and the relationship I didn't have with Brandon, but also for my own mother and the father that never existed in our lives.

"Emma, you'll meet the right guy for you. I just know it."

"Thanks, Jill," I said. "Thanks for listening to me. I'd love to see you girls next weekend if you're all free."

"Don't worry, I'll plan it out," Jill said eagerly.

I couldn't resist a giggle. "You and all your planning."

"I know, right? Why am I an accountant? I should really be an event planner or something." Jill giggled.

"Thanks for being here for me."

"You know I'm always here for you. Just call me whenever you need to talk."

"Thanks. I think I'm going to watch some T.V. and do some things around the apartment."

"Okay, don't think too much about it. Love you."

"Love you too. I'll talk to you soon." I put my phone on silent and laid my head down on my pillow. I was emotionally drained from all that had happened today. I closed my eyes. They were swollen and my head throbbed with pain from all the crying. Thankfully, within minutes, I was drifting in and out of consciousness and quickly fell back into a deep, dreamless sleep.

That was Saturday, and it was Tuesday morning now. I turned my head to look again at the alarm clock. It was 6:59 a.m. It would go off in less than a minute. I took in a deep, anxious breath and tried to let it out slowly as I felt my body sink deeper into my bed. I did not want to get up. I did not want to move, to think, to face the world.

The alarm started buzzing and I moaned. I forced myself out of bed. I had to go to work today. I had called in sick yesterday because I was a mess and wasn't ready to face anyone. But I knew I couldn't afford to call in sick again today. First, I had just started working at Fisher & Morrison a few months ago and did not want to leave a bad impression. Plus, I was just reassigned to another project group last week, and my new group leader Josephine Kim had just given me a few projects on Friday that I haven't had a chance to review yet. I could not lose this job over a guy. And if I was really honest with myself, I also didn't want Brandon to think that he could affect me this way—that he could devastate me and potentially ruin my career. He didn't deserve that power. He had already taken so much away from me, I wasn't going to give him that.

***

By 8:15 a.m., I was outside my apartment building and walking towards the Financial District where Fisher & Morrison Consulting was located. It had rained heavily for most of Sunday and Monday—matching perfectly with my own emotional state. This morning, the air was cool and damp and thin rays of sunlight broke through the dense, grey clouds overhead. I turned towards my left where I could see the Golden Gate Bridge peeking through the fog and a faint rainbow arched over the bay. I laughed to myself at the bitter irony that crossed my mind. My relationship with Brandon was like this rainbow—though it was beautiful and magical, it was uncertain and elusive; there was nothing tangible about it. And as magically as it appeared, it could quickly disappear without warning. Chasing it would be a fool's errand. Chasing after this happily-ever-after with Brandon was my fool's errand.

My heart raced and anxiety coursed through me as I walked out of the elevator and into the lobby of Fisher & Morrison Consulting. Part of me expected him to be standing on the other side of the elevator when it opened, waiting for me. But to my relief, he wasn't there. In fact, I safely got to my desk without bumping into him.

"Hey Emma, are you feeling better?" said a girl with shoulder-length red hair sitting at the workstation next to mine.

"Oh, hi Katie. Yes, I'm feeling better." I gave Katie a small, reassuring smile as guilt prickled inside at my lie. "Did I miss anything important yesterday?"

"Not much. Just the weekly Monday meeting with the other project groups," came a voice behind me. I turned around and saw Steve, a tall, lanky guy with light brown hair who sat at the other end of my workstation. Katie and Steve were the two other associates in my new project group. While I liked Katie and Steve from the Friday happy hours, I realized I didn't really know them. I also wasn't sure how they felt about the fact that they lost George from their project group when I was reassigned to this group and George was reassigned to Brandon's project group.

"Oh yeah, your boyfriend did come by looking for you yesterday," Steve said in a teasing voice.

My heart tightened as his words. "Oh." I wasn't sure how to respond, but I knew I wasn't ready to explain to them why Brandon was no longer my boyfriend. For some reason, explaining to the people at work, who also knew Brandon, seemed to make the end of our short-lived relationship that much more real. I wasn't ready to face that yet. I gave Steve a small smile before turning to my work.

For the rest of the morning, I immersed myself into the two new projects Josephine put me on. I forced myself to be completely absorbed into work so that my thoughts would not drift to the only place it would undoubtedly go.

By 11:25 a.m., I was going through my second binder of financial statements for the Mandoni merger project when I felt my attention waver as I felt a nervousness prickle through me. I wasn't sure why, but I looked up from my desk and looked around. I froze and felt my body stiffen as I saw Brandon looking at me as he approached my workstation. He looked gorgeous; his broad, toned shoulders defined his grey charcoal suit, his tanned, sharp facial features was softened by the deep-set dimples that never failed to make my heart flutter, and his naturally-tousled, dark-brown locks lightly bounced as he walked towards me.

"Emma, can we talk?" Brandon whispered as he leaned over the partition of my workstation.

"I'm not sure that's a good idea," I heard myself say. I felt my heart breaking all over again as I looked at him. I quickly looked away as I tried to think over the pain that pierced through me at the sight of him. I had told myself that I would be strong, that I would brush him off the minute I saw him again. Yet, now with him just inches away from me, I felt my resolution falter.

"Emma, you don't get it—"

"No," I interrupted him, still unable to meet his eyes, "Brandon, we're at work. Just don't. I just can't do this, especially not here." I looked around. I was relieved that Katie and Steve seemed to be engrossed in their work.

"Emma, I just want to talk," he said with a strained voice. The heaviness in his voice caused me to pause. I looked up at him and finally looked into his eyes for the first time since he broke my heart. He looked tired and full of pain, and for a brief moment, my heart ached at the idea that he was also hurting.

"I can't—" I whispered, almost pleading.

"Emma," he interrupted me, "she's my ex."

## CHAPTER TWO

*Brandon*

I watched Emma's expression change from pain to understanding and the tension in my body eased slightly. I needed her to believe me.

"Your ex?" she asked softly as her brilliant, emerald eyes twinkled with moisture. God, she was so beautiful. I reached over and gently brushed away a tear that was rolling down her cheek. Her skin was warm and soft. I looked at her pink, supple lips and I desperately wanted to kiss her.

"Yes. I should have told you when I spoke to you on the phone, but I really had no idea why you were upset. Desiree didn't tell me anything. It didn't dawn on me until you ripped me a new one and called her my girlfriend." I looked at her and smiled.

"I didn't ripped you a new one," she retorted and made a face, and I chuckled. I felt relieved that she was talking to me again.

"Wanna bet?"

"Wait, how could you have thought I would just run out randomly? What did you think I was upset about?"

I thought about it for a moment. I didn't want to tell her what I really thought. I didn't want to admit that I thought that Des had told her something about our past, about our history—something I didn't want Emma to know about. Des and I had a long and complicated past, but it was all in the past and I wanted my future with Emma in it. If she knew everything about Des and me, I wasn't sure how she'd react. I didn't want her to think less of me, and I definitely wasn't about to risk losing her over it.

I looked at Emma and smiled. "I really didn't know why you were upset. That's why I kept stalking you with all my calls, texts, and the drop-by," I teased, avoiding her question.

Emma gave a tiny smile and I knew she wasn't quite convinced, but she kept quiet. *Thank God, I wasn't ready for this conversation.* That was one of the endearing qualities that I loved about her. I knew she was insightful, but she knew when to ask a question and when not to push it. I wasn't perfect, and one of my biggest pet peeves was being pushed to answer something I wasn't ready to answer.

"So are we okay?" I asked.

"I'm not sure, Brandon. I think I need time to process this," she said softly.

"Oh." I felt disappointment twist at my stomach and my muscles tensed. I wanted us to get over this awkwardness already. I wanted everything to go back to how it was before Des ruined everything. I looked at my watch. "Well, it's 11:45 a.m. If you're up for it, we can go grab lunch in 15 or even 45 minutes if that's enough time for you. We can talk more about what happened and I'll let you know why Desiree is in town." She looked at me and I saw the spark of interest in her eyes. I smiled. I planned to tell her about Desiree; I planned to tell her everything she needed to know and nothing more.

***

The sky had cleared since this morning and the sun was shining overhead. A few white, puffy clouds floated lazily through the sky. The autumn air smelled fresh and crisp, soothing the tension I felt inside. A light wind blew past us as we walked down the pier, causing Emma's long, blonde hair to dance gently with the breeze, brushing against her face like thin strands of gold thread. I looked over at her, and without thinking, I reached over and brushed a few strands of her hair behind her ear. It felt natural—like something I was born to do. Even in this moment where things were uncertain between us, I felt connected to her, almost like an invisible string that permanently connected our souls to one another. I was happier and more carefree when she was near. She felt like home.

She smiled up at me, and I felt my heart beat faster. I knew she was nervous, and I felt the same nerves too. I wanted our discussion to go well. I wanted her to look at me in that sweet, endearing way that only she could do. I wanted her to continue to fall in love with me. I wanted—no, I needed her innocent and unadulterated love. She gave herself to me like she'd never given to another man; I was her first. I wished I had been able to give her the same.

But I couldn't; I no longer had that to give because it was given to Desiree many years ago.

"What are you thinking?" Emma looked at me, and there was a hint of worry in her eyes.

"Nothing. Not much." I gave her one of my smiles, hoping it would relax her. "I was just thinking that's a nice spot for our lunch." I gestured to an empty bench that faced the water overlooking the Bay Bridge. It had turned out to be a nice day out, so we had decided to get some sandwiches from a food truck and find a nice spot outside to talk.

"Sure," she said as she smiled at me. I could never get tired of that smile.

"Emma, I don't want things to be awkward between us," I said as we sat down on the bench. I faced her and held her hand with mine. "I really care about you. I really hope you know that. You have no idea how miserable I've been since you ran out of my place Saturday morning."

"So why didn't you run after me?" she asked quickly. She looked away from me, and it killed me that she was still hurt, that I was the one who caused that pain.

"I tried. I …"

She looked at me in confusion. "What do you mean you tried? How exactly did you do that?" There was an edge of bitterness in her voice, and it frightened me that she may not forgive me.

"I tried to go after you, but when I got down to the lobby, I saw you leaving in a cab." Guilt filled me as I explained the half-truth. I had gone looking for her that morning, but Des had first stopped me. She said that Emma would be fine and that she probably left because something had came up. I hadn't believed her, but somehow Des convinced me to stay a few minutes longer to catch up with her. She complained that I hadn't seen her in months and with our history, she deserved more from me. She was probably right. Des deserved more, and I have been filled with guilt knowing that I couldn't give her what she wanted. When I finally got to the lobby 10 minutes later, I thought Emma was long gone. I was surprised to actually catch her getting into that cab. *Had she been waiting for me to chase after her? Was that her intention?*

"So ..." Emma interrupted my thoughts. "Is she really your ex?"

"Yes. Absolutely," I said with conviction. "We are not together anymore."

"So why did she stop by that morning? Does she do that often?"

I could sense the jealousy in her voice, and a part of me was thrilled to know that she was jealous. It meant she still wanted to be with me. "No, she doesn't stop by often—actually rarely. She lives in LA. I didn't know she was in town this past weekend and I wasn't expecting her to stop by unannounced. She shouldn't have done that. I'm not sure exactly what she told you, but she's not my girlfriend. I hope you believe me." I looked at her expectantly, hoping we could put all this behind us.

"I do believe you," she said softly as she looked up at me. Our eyes locked and I felt the undeniable attraction between us.

I leaned down and gently kissed her soft, sweet lips. "I've missed you," I whispered. "I'm really sorry she stopped by and said what she said to you. I don't like seeing you hurt. I would do anything to take it back if I could. I hate that I'm the one that caused you any pain."

She kissed me back and whispered, "I'm scared, Brandon."

"Of what?" I didn't understand her statement and anxiety shot through me.

"I was really hurt when I thought that she was your girlfriend—that you loved someone else. I felt stupid and embarrassed that I was the other woman. And that really hurt. I'm scared because I know that if you can cause me this kind of pain now, I'm not sure I will survive the pain you would cause when I fall harder for you. And I will fall harder for you if I continue to see you."

My hand reached for her face and I pulled her closer to me. The visible pain in her eyes gnawed at my heart. "I don't want you to be scared to be with me. I would never intentionally hurt you, Emma. I really want this to work between us. Desiree is a part of my past and I can't change that, but you are who I want to be with—my present and my future. Just give me a chance to prove that to you."

There were tears in her eyes and she looked up at me with a look of hope and gently nodded. Relief washed through me and I pulled her into my arms and she buried her face into my chest. I embraced her tightly and kissed her forehead. "Thank you," I whispered. "You mean more to me than you know." I meant it. I hadn't known it at the time, but I had fallen in love with her during the first night we met. I couldn't explain why, but there was something about her.

I felt myself gravitate towards her. Her pure innocence and sincerity drew me in and made me want to stay with her forever. I felt carefree when I was with her. I wanted to be a better man for her. And above all, she made me laugh. I couldn't remember the last time I truly laughed before meeting her.

"Brandon?" Emma looked up from under my arms. "Can you tell me something?"

"Of course." I felt my body stiffen at her question.

"Can you tell me about her?"

"About Desiree?" I didn't feel like delving into the past, and this was not the conversation I wanted to have right now.

"Yes." She looked at me tentatively. "I just want to know a little more about your relationship with her. I just don't understand why she would just show up at your place unannounced. I need you to help me understand your relationship with her."

"I understand. I really do," I said, trying to stall as I thought about what I wanted to tell her. I wasn't ready to tell her everything, and she didn't need to know everything. "Well, Des and I were high school sweethearts." I paused before admitting, "And we were each other's first love."

I saw the unease in Emma's face at those words. "It was puppy love," I explained. "We were young and we were there for one another during that time. But when we graduated high school, I moved to Boston for college and she moved to L.A. We tried to stay together, but we grew apart." I paused and looked at Emma. She was deep in thought, and I wished I knew what she was thinking.

"How long were you guys together for?"

"We started dating at the beginning of our junior year in high school. We did the long-distance dating thing all through college, but I'm not sure that counted. We broke up a number of times and barely saw each other. We also casually dated other people between each break-up."

"When was the last time you guys were together?"

I thought about my answer before saying, "We officially broke up shortly after we graduated from college. Our relationship during college was rocky. We were long distance the entire time, and with summer internships and studying abroad, we never saw each other for more than a week or two at time."

"So when was that?"

I wasn't sure why she wanted to know the details, and I didn't want to talk about it anymore. "Um, about three years ago."

"So why was she in town? I still don't get it."

"Emma, I really don't want to talk about the past. I want to talk about us and our relationship." I wanted her to drop this line of questioning. I wanted her to see me the way she did before Des showed up.

"Brandon, I need to know. I'm sorry if I'm prying, but please see this from my perspective. I've had one of the worst few days of my life after the best night of my life with you. I need to understand why your ex would just show up at your place and tell me she's your girlfriend. You owe me at least that."

I could hear the hurt in her voice, and feelings of guilt and fear washed over me. I wanted to tell her everything, but I was afraid that if I did, she would never look at me the way she used to—like I was the perfect man who could do no wrong, like I was the *one* for her. I wanted—no, I needed her to look at me that way.

"Emma, I do want to tell you everything—"

"So are you saying that you're not telling me everything?"

I took a deep breath. How am I going to explain this? "No, that's not what I was saying. Emma, please understand that I do have a long history with Des. She was there for me when I went through a dark period of my life during high school. Well recently, she was going through some things of her own, and I knew I needed to be there for her. She didn't have anyone else to turn to."

"Oh," she said quietly and her expression softened. "What dark period of your life? Is she okay?"

I looked at her with pleading eyes. I wanted this to be a happy lunch for us, not something so heavy. I didn't want to think about my past, about a time when I was at my lowest. But I knew I had to tell her. If I wanted to keep Emma in my life, I had to fight against my urge to close her out and share my pain with her. I took both her hands and squeezed it. She looked at me with concern and love, and I realized how much I needed her in my life—how much I needed her innocence and love.

"This was not how I had wanted to tell you about this part of my past. I haven't shared this with many people. Actually, I haven't told anyone who didn't already know because they were in my life during that time." I paused and looked at her, and the reassuring look in her eyes made me feel more relaxed.

I took a deep breath before continuing, "I lost my mom when I was 16." My heart twisted in pain from saying this out loud, from admitting it had happened. It had been almost 11 years since I've lost her, but time had not made it easier. Time had not healed those wounds.

"Oh, Brandon. I'm so sorry," Emma whispered softly and I saw the sadness in her eyes. She pulled me into her arms and hugged me, and I felt myself relax in the security of her embrace—in the security of her pure love, a place where sadness did not exist. "What happened?" There was no pity in her voice, just unadulterated concern and sadness, and I felt my feelings for this beautiful woman deepen.

"She died from breast cancer." I felt a surge of emotions surface inside me. "The doctors discovered the lump the year before she passed away, but at that point, it was too late. The cancer had spread to other parts of her body, and the doctors said it was terminal and that she only had up to a year to live."

"That's awful." Tears welled up in Emma's eyes, and it pained me to cause her more tears.

"Yeah, it was," I whispered as I thought about my mother. "My mom was one of the most amazing women I've ever known. Everything good about who I am today was because of her and how she raised me. I wish she knew how much she meant to me."

"Brandon, I'm sure she knew," Emma said softly as her hand rubbed my back.

"She had convinced my dad not to tell me right away about the cancer. She didn't want death to be what our family thought about during her last days with us. She wanted us to think only about love. She gave me so much love during the last year of her life while she was in pain, and I didn't even know. I didn't know until they rushed her into the hospital due to internal bleeding. I didn't know until the last week of her life that she was dying. I didn't even get the chance to show her how much I loved her." Tears blinded my vision as I relived the darkest days of my life. I felt Emma's gentle hands brushed against my cheeks as she pulled me into her embrace. I buried my face into the contours of her neck and hair and inhaled her comforting scent.

"I'm so sorry, Brandon. I'm sure she knew you loved her very much. She sounds like an amazing person."

"She was. Losing her was the hardest thing I've gone through. My dad tried to be there for me, but he was going through his own grief over my mom. I went into a deep depression and shut the world out for a very long time."

We remained silent for awhile as I relived those memories in my mind.

"So, was that when you met Desiree?" Emma asked tentatively. I could hear the discomfort in her voice when she said Des's name.

"We had just started dating a few months before my mom passed away. She had refused to let me shut her out and was there for me. For the longest time, she was the only one I really spoke to outside of school. In a way, she saved my life."

"I see," Emma said softly. I saw the anguish in her face.

"Emma, this is why I didn't want to tell you about this so soon. Des was there for me and I will always be indebted to her for not giving up on me when I was at my lowest. Recently, she was going through some tough times of her own, and I wanted to be there for her. I do still love her and care about her, but as a *friend*." I emphasized the last word, hoping that Emma could understand and accept this. "Emma, there's nothing you need to worry about between Des and me."

I leaned down and kissed her lips. "She may be an important part of my world, but I want you to be in the center of my world."

"I'm not sure what to say. This is a lot to take in." Her face was a mixture of emotions that I couldn't quite understand.

"I know," I said with a nod. "I'm sorry I didn't tell you this sooner, but we haven't known each other for that long and I wanted you to get to know me for me, and not me with my past."

"I understand. And I'm sorry I didn't let you explain things sooner and ran out. I was just so hurt when I saw her. She's gorgeous, she showed up unannounced at your place on a Saturday morning, and she said she was your girlfriend. There was no reason for me to doubt the truth of her words."

I felt a wave of anger for Des and the mess she had caused. "Don't apologize. There's nothing you should be sorry for. I'm sorry you had to meet her that way. I didn't realized she told you she was my girlfriend. She kept denying she said anything. We broke up three years ago. I know it's not an excuse, but she's going through a lot right now. We dated for eight years, and sometimes, I'm not sure if she has completely accepted the fact that we're not together anymore."

"Yeah, it doesn't seem like she has," Emma agreed. Her voice was even, and I could tell she was trying to hide her feelings from me.

"Hey," I squeezed her arms lightly, "that doesn't matter. I told her about you and she knows that we're together—at least I hope we're still together." I looked at her for affirmation.

She nodded with a small smile, and I felt a huge weight of anxiety lift from my shoulders. I was relieved that we're finally moving on from this misunderstand.

"Hey, I'm really sorry for putting you through all this. I know I caused you a lot of pain. I want to do something special for you."

"Oh, you don't have to. Just don't hurt me again, and I'll be happy." She gave me a smile that masked the pain I could see that I had caused.

*Man, she was too sweet and forgiving.* I pulled her in for another kiss—this time, our lips lingered and we explored each other with a rushed eagerness. I almost forgot how much I missed her lips; they were soft and sweet, and instantly, I wished the pier wasn't full with the lunch crowd rush walking past us.

"What are you doing after work today?" I asked brightly. I wanted to show her how much I cared about her. I wanted to plan something romantic for her. I wanted her to know how sorry I was for causing her so much pain.

"Honestly, I haven't thought that far ahead. When I got up for work today, this wasn't how I anticipated the day to go," she said.

"Well, I hope it's better than what you had anticipated."

"Definitely," she laughed.

Then her expression immediately changed and became serious. "Don't hurt me again," she said in a serious tone as she gently hit my arm.

I smiled at her. "I won't. I promise." I kissed her again, trying to reassure her that I meant it, trying to reassure myself that I wouldn't. I would not be able to live with myself if I hurt her again. I pushed away those thought. "Well, if you're free, can I stop by after work? Let's say 7 p.m.? I need to pick up a few things, but I can pick up some dinner and we can hang out. How does that sound?"

"It sounds nice," she smiled—a smile that put a smile on my face. "Just one problem," she continued.

My body tensed. "What?"

"I'm not sure I trust you with food, so don't bring over dinner. I'll cook." Her playfulness made me laughed and it was this same playfulness that I loved and felt at ease with.

"Deal. Even though you almost burned down my place last time with that *au jus* sauce, I'll put my life in your hands and let you cook," I teased back.

We smiled and looked at each other in silence, and for a brief moment, the hubbub of other people on the pier became muffled and distance, and all that mattered was Emma. Emma and me. Together.

***

I heard my phone go off in the bedroom as I stepped out of the shower. *Maybe it was Emma*, I thought with a smile. Emma had texted a few times after work to figure out what we'd be having for dinner. I was pretty sure we had decided on some curry butter chicken thing. I think I've had that once at an Indian restaurant. She also mentioned some grilled asparagus with cheese or something. I've had grilled asparagus and enjoyed it, but I didn't have the heart to question her about the cheese part, or about grilled asparagus with Indian food. *Maybe I should stop by McDonald's on the way there just to be on the safe side.*

I shaved and slapped on some aftershave before getting dressed. I wanted tonight to be special. I've already picked up the things I needed on my way home. I hope she'll enjoy everything. I loved her genuine surprise and joy when I planned our first night together on the terrace. I was surprised at just how happy her reaction had made me.

Just then my phone went off again. *It must be Emma again.* I looked around for my phone, trying to remember where I last left it. I followed the sound, and finally found it in the breast pocket of the suit that was laid out on the leather recliner next to my bed. I quickly picked up the phone and answered before it could go to voicemail. "Hey, sorry, I couldn't find my phone," I said breathlessly. "Sorry, I think I'll be a few minutes later, but I'm heading over now. Don't eat all the curry butter chicken." I laughed.

My laughed came to an abrupt stop when I heard the voice that came from the other end of the phone.

"Were you expecting someone else?"

It was Desiree.

"Oh, hi Des." *Why was she calling?*

"Wow, don't try to sound too excited to hear from me," she said flatly.

"I'm sorry, Des, but after the mess you made by telling Emma you're my girlfriend, I'm not really in the mood to talk to you. Besides, I'm in a hurry. What's up?" I tried my best to sound patient.

"In a hurry?" she asked as she ignored everything else I said. "Let me guess? Are you going to go see that girl?"

I felt annoyed by Desiree's dismissiveness. "If you mean Emma, then yes, I am. I'm dating her, Des. I'm happy. I hope you can understand that."

There was silence on the other line.

"Des? Why did you call? Do you need something?" I tried to keep my voice even, devoid of my growing irritation.

"Well, I was just calling to let you know that I'll be heading back to L.A. tomorrow and wanted to see if you wanted to grab breakfast before I left town."

"Des, I have work tomorrow. You know that."

"I do, but you're also the boss, you don't have to be there right on time. Consider it a breakfast meeting."

I sighed. Des was always a persistent person. It was that same persistence that had saved me those many years ago when I tried to shut everyone out as I mourned over my mother. The persistence that had saved me from falling too far into the abyss of the depression I had been spiraling down towards. And for that, I was thankful. "Okay, Des," I sighed, "Just a short breakfast."

"Awesome!" she said excitedly, "Oh, and I have some exciting news to share!"

## CHAPTER THREE
### *Emma*

The intercom buzzed and I smiled. *That must be Brandon.*

"Hi," I said into the intercom.

"Hey you, it's me. Are you going to buzz me in this time?" he asked teasingly.

"Careful there, or I won't," I teased back and then pressed the button to let Brandon through the lobby door downstairs. Excitement shot through me as I waited for Brandon to come up from the lobby. I thought about how much of a difference 24 hours could make and laughed at myself. It had all been a misunderstanding. Desiree was his ex, and *I* was his girlfriend. I smiled and realized how much I had overreacted.

A knock on the door brought me out of my thoughts. I went to open it and was greeted with a bouquet of rich dark pink peonies and Brandon standing there with a gorgeous wide smile.

"Hi," I said breathlessly, "those are beautiful! How did you know I love peonies? These aren't even in season."

"I have my ways," Brandon said teasingly and he gave me a warm hug and kissed my right cheek.

*Must be Sarah*, I thought. "Thanks. You're too sweet." I took the peonies from him and found a vase to put them in.

"So this is your place," Brandon said from somewhere behind me.

I turned around and blushed with embarrassment as I also looked around my tiny studio apartment and thought of Brandon's amazing condo that was probably 20 times the size of this place. "Yeah, it's not much, but it's close to work."

"No, I didn't mean it that way." Brandon smiled. "I meant, I like it, it feels like you." He looked at me warmly.

"What do you mean by that?"

"Well, it's homey and filled with signs of love," he said as he walked the few steps towards my bookshelf and looked at the photos of me with my mom and friends. "It's a reflection of who you are," he said as he looked up at me. "You don't seem to know it, but you have a way of making people feel comfortable around you and you give people a lot of love." He smiled at me in a way that took my breath away.

"Thanks." I was touched by his words and filled with a wave of emotions to hear the way he thought of me.

"Is this your mom?" Brandon asked.

"Yeah," I said as I saw the picture of my mom and me at my graduation commencement ceremony. I smiled at the memory of that day. Besides my move-in day freshman year, that was the only time my mom visited me on campus. She lived in Sacramento, which was a six to seven hour drive to Los Angeles, and she could not afford to take off that much time from work. I loved my mom and wished she could have visited more often so we could spend more time together. But I knew she had a lot of debt from the all the years of raising me as a single mom. So when she visited L.A. for my graduation, it meant a lot to me that she was there, and that picture reminded me of everything she had done for me in my life.

"I don't see any pictures of your dad." Brandon's comment pulled me from my thoughts and a wave of sadness hit me. He looked over at me and saw the pain in my eyes and immediately said, "I'm sorry, Emma. I didn't mean to …"

"It's okay. You're right, there isn't a picture of my father." I paused. "I actually don't know what he looks like. He was never a part of my life." I looked away from Brandon as tears filled my eyes. I walked over to the stove to remove the chicken out of the oven where it had been warming.

"I'm sorry, Emma," came Brandon's voice from behind me and I felt him gently put his arms around me from behind. I turned around to face him and I saw the concern in his warm, brown eyes. "I didn't mean to … do you want to talk about?"

"It's okay, but I don't really want to talk about it right now. Is that okay?" I was not ready to talk about the father that was never a part of my life. A man who I had hated for so long.

"Of course," he said softly as he leaned down and kissed my forehead. He pulled away and smiled at me—a smile that had a way of melting away my sadness. "Only happy thoughts tonight, okay?"

"Deal." I smiled, grateful that he hadn't pushed me to tell him more about my father. I wasn't ready to go through that emotional roller coaster. Not tonight.

"Wow, I'm excited about this curry butter chicken thing. It smells amazing," he said excitedly. "I think I've had it once at a restaurant, though I'm not sure it looked like that," he said as he suspiciously eyed the dish.

I frowned. "Oh? You have?" This was a simple home-style chicken recipe. I wouldn't expect to see it served in a restaurant. "Did you like it?"

"Yeah, it was pretty good. I'm impressed you know how to cook Indian food."

I looked at him in confusion. "What do you mean? How do you know I can cook Indian food?"

"Because you just made it. The curry butter chicken."

I started laughing when I realized what Brandon must have meant. Brandon looked at me in confusion. "What did I say?"

"I think you thought I was making butter chicken, which is an Indian dish. But I made a baked chicken with a mixture of honey, butter, and curry powder. It's not an Indian dish at all," I said between giggles.

"Oh." Brandon began to laugh too. "That makes more sense."

"How so?"

"Well I was wondering why you'd make an Indian dish and grilled asparagus in the same meal."

We both laughed.

"That's what you get for doubting me," I teased.

"I guess you learn something new every day," he said teasingly as he pulled me into his hard, warm chest and kissed me. "Now let's eat."

***

After a delicious meal, Brandon suggested watching a movie. I ended up picking some random action flick on Netflix, something I thought we could both enjoy. After a few minutes into the movie, Brandon got up to use the restroom.

"Do you want me to pause the film?" I asked.

"No, that's okay. I'll be back in a bit." He leaned over the couch to kiss me. "Don't miss me too much," he teased.

I rolled my eyes and giggled.

When 10 minutes had passed and Brandon still hadn't returned from the restroom, I was starting to wonder if he was okay. I couldn't really hear anything from the bathroom over the noise of the TV, but I thought I heard the water running. *Maybe he's making a call*, I thought. *Maybe he's calling Desiree*, a tiny voice whispered inside my head. "No," I heard myself say out loud. "Stop jumping to conclusion again, Emma." I shook my head, as if I could shake off that jealous thought.

"Sorry to interrupt." I jumped at the sound of Brandon's voice.

"Oh. Sorry." *God, he must have heard me talking to myself.* I felt my face grow hot as I looked over at him. "How much did you hear?" I asked sheepishly.

"Nothing at all," Brandon said with a smirk. I cringed with embarrassment.

"Is everything okay?" I asked, trying to change the subject.

Brandon raised his eyebrows. "Why wouldn't it be?"

"You were just, um, just in the bathroom for a while," I replied hesitantly.

Brandon laughed. "Right. Well, I had some business to take care of."

"Gross," I said, making a face of disgust as I laughed.

Brandon shrugged and laughed. "Come over here. I need to show you something."

I looked at him and felt uneasy. "What did you do?" I asked tentatively. *Oh God, did he clog my toilet?* I thought. *I am not ready for that type of intimacy. In fact, I never want to be ready for that sort of intimacy.*

"Just come over here already," he said with a playful air of impatience. "Or else, I'll have to make you come over here." There was something raw and forceful in his voice that instantly turned me on.

"And what if I want you to make me come to you," I flirted back as I slowly got up from the couch. Our eyes locked on to one another and I instantly knew he was turned on too.

When I got close enough, he grabbed my waist and pulled me urgently towards him and whispered hotly into my ear, "I would have had a lot of fun making you come … to me."

I gasped at his bold suggestive statement; his hot breathe in my ear stirred a familiar desire in the pit of my stomach. I was beyond turned on. Without a second thought, I grabbed his gorgeous face with both hands and pulled him down towards me. I was desperate for his lips on mine—I yearned to taste him and for him to taste me. When his mouth enveloped mine, I felt an electric current pulse between our connection. My lips moved against his eagerly, and with every growing second, they were hungry for more of him. His tongue parted me and I eagerly took him in. As our kiss deepen, I felt the hardness grow in his jeans as his hands brushed through my hair and explored my back.

"I want you now," I said in a ragged whisper as I tried to pull him toward my bed on the opposite end of the room.

Brandon resisted my movement towards the bed and gently pulled away from me. "God, you have no idea how much I want you, Emma, but—"

"Actually, I do," I purred, interrupting him and rubbed my hand against the ever-growing bulge that pressed against his jeans on the other side.

Brandon groaned, "Don't tempt me, Emma, or I won't be able to hold back any longer if you do."

I was about to protest, but he held his hand to my lips. "I want to show you something first." He gestured to the closed bathroom door, and it wasn't until then that I remember why I got up from the couch in the first place.

"Ok, what is it?" I asked uncertainly. I thought about what he must have been doing in the bathroom just minutes ago and I grimaced.

"Open the door and you'll find out," he prompted as he stood behind me facing the door. I looked back at him with confusion and he chuckled. I turned to the door to open it, and was prepared to hold my breath to avoid smelling anything. But instead, I gasped. Two dozen candles of various sizes were lit around my bathroom, their reflection danced against the white, porcelain-tile walls surrounding the clawfoot bathtub. The bathtub was filled to the brim with rich layers of bubbles. The air was steamy and an inviting aroma of lavender oil greeted my nose.

I turned around to look at him, "You did all this?"

He nodded and smiled. He walked over to a small portable radio on the sink and turned it on. Soft jazz music began to play seductively as he turned to me and gave me a breath-taking smile. "I wanted to do something special for you to help you relax."

I felt my body melt at the pleasant surprise. "Wow, you're too good to be true."

"I will take that as a compliment," he teased.

I laughed and then paused. "But where did all this come from?" I asked. "I don't remember you bringing any of this stuff with you tonight."

Brandon chuckled, "That's because I was stealthy."

I laughed. "No really, how did you sneak this all in?"

"You were just too distracted by my charm, good looks, and body. I could seriously get anything by you," he continued to tease.

I hit his arm playfully. "Tell me," I demanded.

"Ouch, don't hurt me," Brandon faked a grimace and then gave an exaggerated sigh. "Okay, if you really must know, you were busy with the flowers when I arrived, so you didn't see me holding a bag, and when you went to the kitchen to get a vase, I put the bag in the bathtub."

I made a feigned expression of hurt on my face, "So you're telling me the flowers were a decoy?"

"Hey, don't say it like that. They came from the heart," Brandon said between fits of laughter as he pressed one hand against his chest. "But," dragging out the word, "I do have to admit, they were convenient."

I laughed and shook my head as I rolled my eyes. I then looked at the inviting bathtub and smiled. "This is so sweet of you."

"I try." He pulled me into his embrace and gently kissed my forehead.

Then, I realized something and I started to laugh.

"What's so funny?" he asked as he gave me a curious look of amusement.

"Well, I have to admit that earlier, when you were in here for such a long time, I was wondering what you must have been doing in here." Then I laughed again and gave him a teasing frown, "I was feeling a little uncomfortable that you had quickly gotten *that* comfortable with me."

Brandon laughed when he realized what I was implying. "But isn't being comfortable with one another a good thing?" he cajoled as he playfully pulled me towards him again for a hug.

"Well, there's comfortable, and then there's *too* comfortable." I laughed.

"Touché. Look at you, always thinking the worst of me."

I stopped laughing and looked up at him, "I'm sorry, Brandon."

"Emma, I was just teasing."

"I know that. What I meant was—"

"Emma, you don't need to explain," he said, interrupting my attempt at an apology. "I just want you to enjoy this bubble bath before the water gets cold. Don't let all my hard work go to waste," he teased.

"Aren't you going to join me?" I asked, hoping he would say yes. Before he could respond, I gave him a devious smile and started pulling off his t-shirt over his head. I wasn't about to let him say no.

He chuckled when I started unbuttoning his jeans. "Well, this was really just supposed to be for you, and for you to relax." He then gave an exaggerated huff and said in a serious tone, "But I *guess* sacrifices must be made in the call of duty." He pushed down his jeans and kicked them to the side.

I giggled, "Life must be so hard for you, Mr. Fisher." I slowly ran my fingers first down his hard, smooth pecks, then down his ripped six-pack abs, and then slowly back up and across his broad muscular shoulders.

"I know," he said in a slow and ragged voice. "It's not every day you're forced to get in a bathtub with the naked hot girl of your dreams." He pulled me towards his half-naked body and I felt his hard erection against my thigh, which ignited a growing need at the pit of my stomach.

"Who said I was going to be naked?" I laughed.

"I did," Brandon said as he pulled my shirt off me. Then his lips and tongue gently traced an invisible line across my bared neck and shoulders as he slowly pulled down my bra straps. A second later, I felt my bra fall to the ground and I inhaled sharply as his wet lips found their way to one of my breast as his hand kneaded the other. My body arched against his touch as my hands grabbed tightly onto his rich, brown hair, urging for him lower to explore more of me.

Brandon looked up at me, his eyes glinting with sparks of desire. "Let's slow it down." His voice was ragged and I knew he didn't mean it.

As if confirming my thoughts, he unzipped my jeans and pulled them down my legs. His face lingered in front of my panties as he breathed me in. "The things I could do to you, Emma." I could hear the need and restraint in his voice, and I felt all my blood rushing down between my legs, towards the exact spot that was currently inches away from his lips. I moaned as I felt his hot breath on my inner thigh. He slowly pulled down my panties and looked up at me, his smoldering, brown eyes were wild with hot intensity.

"I need you now," I begged as I backed up against the wall and spread my legs wider, desperate for a part of him to be inside of me. He gently ran his fingertips up the inner parts of my leg towards my pleasure spot, sending a shiver down my spine. I felt two of his rough, skilled fingers enter me and I cried out in pleasure.

"Fuck, you're so wet," he groaned. He moved his fingers in and out of me with increasing momentum as his tongue explored and tasted me. My body convulsed as the ripples of pleasure built inside me. "God, Brandon. I'm about to come," I moaned.

"Yes, come for me, baby," he growled as he watched my body quiver with pleasure.

"But ... but I want you inside me. I want you to come with me." My voice was shaky and I gasped each time his fingers entered me, each time a little deeper and more forceful than the last.

"Don't worry. We'll have time for that." I met his wild, intense gaze as I felt my body spasm into ecstasy. "Oh. God. Brandon," I screamed as my body tightened around his fingers as waves of bliss crashed through me. Finally, I felt my body grow limp as I held onto him.

"I love it when you come." Brandon grinned as he slowly removed his fingers from inside me and licked them, his eyes never leaving mine. "Now let's get you in that bathtub before I can't bear it anymore and take you against the bathroom wall."

Even in the fog of my delirious comedown from pleasure, I was turned on by his words and wanted every inch of him to be inside me—deep inside me. My breath caught as I watched his manhood spring out into view as he pulled down his boxer brief. He was very hard. He was very ready. I felt myself tighten in anticipation below. I was ready for him.

We stepped into the tub and as I sunk into the hot water, I sighed as I felt my body instantly relax. Brandon faced me from the other side of the tub and our legs entangled around each other. We smiled at each other, and I realized how happy he made me.

"You're amazing, Brandon Fisher," I whispered. "Thank you for being you."

"It's easy to be myself when I'm with you, Emma."

I shook my head in disagreement, "You don't give yourself enough credit. You're so patient with me, even when I've thought the worst of you. I'm really sorry for being so melodramatic when Desiree showed up at your place the other morning." I looked at him, hoping he can see the regret in my eyes.

"Emma, you have nothing to apologize for." His warm, brown eyes were inviting and sincere, and I felt myself fall even deeper for him. *How is he so forgiving? How is he so perfect?*

"But I do," I corrected him. "I'm sorry for not believing in you—in us. For running out that morning without giving you a chance to explain. For automatically believing in her when she claimed she was your girlfriend." I paused and felt tears well up in my eyes as a flood of emotions washed through me as I grappled at my words. "I should have at least heard your side of the story instead of running away and ignoring you. I totally overreacted, and I feel ashamed for not believing in you, especially when you haven't given me any reason to doubt you."

There was a look in Brandon's eyes that I couldn't understand. *Would he truly forgive me for being such a drama queen?*

"Emma, it's in the past. I'm just glad that we got everything cleared up."

"I know, but I do owe you an apology. You've been nothing but good to me. I'm sorry for being so immature sometimes. I just have a hard time trusting people, especially men, and I'm sorry I didn't trust you. You didn't deserve that from me."

"It's okay, Emma. I understand where you're coming from," Brandon said softly. "You've had some bad run-ins with men in the past, so I get it. And your reaction was completely understandable. If it makes you feel any better, you're the only person I would want showing up unannounced at my place, and preferably in a trench coat and nothing else," he smiled and gave me a wink.

"Thanks," I laughed. I loved how easygoing he was and how comfortable he made me feel. "I'll keep that in mind next time I stop by your place unannounced."

"Looking forward to it," he said.

The flames from the candles twinkled in his eyes as he stared at me. His facial feature were chiseled and defined, softened by those deep, gorgeous dimples that made my body melt. He had moments earlier combed through his dark, brown locks with his hands, leaving them brushed back and partially wet, making him look incredibly sexy. I sighed as I took the image of him in. He was perfect—beyond handsome— and he wanted to be with me.

"What are you thinking?" he asked, bringing me out of my reverie.

"I … I was just wondering if you, um, played the guitar," I managed to finally say. I wasn't going to admit that I was admiring his sexiness and wondering why he wanted to be with me.

"The guitar?" He looked at me with amusement. "Why? Do you have a thing for guys playing the guitar?"

I laughed, "A little. I guess the image of you in a guitar just popped into my head, and I was curious." He didn't have to know the image of him playing a guitar came from a dream-turned-nightmare I recently of him.

"Sorry kid, but your boyfriend doesn't know how to play a guitar. Worst boyfriend ever, I know," he teased.

"Darn, so you're not perfect after all," I feigned a look of disappointment.

Brandon chuckled. "Maybe someday. Maybe someday I'll surprise you and play the guitar for you."

"Well if you tell me, then how is that a surprise?"

"Be nice."

I giggled. I smiled at him. "Hey, are you free next weekend?"

"Thanksgiving weekend?"

I nodded.

"Yeah, I think so. My dad and I usually go to my aunt's house in Sausalito, a little north of here, for Thanksgiving dinner. I don't have anything else planned. Why?"

"Well, my three best friends will be in town that weekend. I'd love for you to meet them."

"Of course. I definitely want to meet your best friends. You've mentioned them a lot in the last couple of months, I feel like I already know them."

"I know they'll love you. I'm really excited about their visit."

I thought about the turn of events and was happy that everything worked out. I had called the girls when I got home from work earlier tonight and told them what happened. I was happy and relieved that our first reunion since graduation wouldn't involve me moping over Brandon having a girlfriend, but would be the first time they got to meet Brandon, my boyfriend.

I smiled at the thought and looked over at Brandon. There was glint in his eyes that made me catch my breath. Then I saw him smile. "What are you thinking?"

"You are unbelievably hot right now." His voice was deep. Primal.

I gave him my most seductive smile. "You're not too bad yourself." I moved my feet under the water towards his inner thigh.

"Emma," he groaned. "You have no idea how crazy you make me. It's taking me all my concentration to not take you now."

"What's stopping you?" I urged. I wanted him to take me now and have his way with me.

"Because I want tonight to be about you, to be about me pleasuring you."

"Well, it would bring me a lot of pleasure if you were inside me," I purred.

Brandon chuckled. "I have no doubt," he paused and a devious smile curled his lips.

Although I couldn't see his erection through the layers of bubbles, I knew that it was long and hard for me right now, and the only things separating us was the water. I felt a growing need course through me at the thought of him inside me. I felt his hands slowly running the length of my legs under the water—from my ankles to my inner thighs where his hands lingered for a moment before moving back towards my ankles. Our eyes met and I was transfixed by the intensity in his eyes as he looked at me. We moved towards each other, meeting in the center of the tub. Our lips met with urgency as I straddled him, feeling his manhood against my skin. His lips left mine and began to taste the spots on my neck that sent currents of pleasure down to towards the spot between my inner thighs. A moan escaped through my lips as my hips rocked against him, needing him to be inside of me.

"I should get a condom now," he whispered.

I shook my head and pulled his face closer towards me. "No, I'm on the pill," I whispered in his ear. "I don't want to use a condom. I want to feel you." I let out a pleading moan, desperate for him to pound inside me; to end this unquenchable need that seems to gnaw at me until he was inside me. "I want to feel every inch of you inside me."

He turned to look at me, his eyes were wild and piercing. "Are you sure?"

My lips twisted into a smile as I moved my hand slowly moved down his chest and explored downward. I followed the triangular lines of his lower ab muscles that led me to his erection. It was satiny hard and ready. My hands moved up and down his length, causing him to throw his head back and groan in pleasure. Intense waves of pleasure throbbed down inside me in anticipation of him entering me. "I'm very sure," I finally answered and guided him deep inside me in one urgent movement.

I heard his sharp inhale of breathe and I smiled wickedly at him. His hand griped onto my back and dug into my skin as he growled in pleasure. "My God, Emma. You feel *so* fucking amazing." I gasped as he grabbed my hips and drove into me deeper and harder. I held onto his broad, defined shoulders, my nails dug into his back as I moved in time with his thrusts. I began to spasm and my inner muscles tightened their grip on his manhood, and I saw the raw pleasure glisten in his eyes.

"God, I'm going to come, Emma." He drove into me harder and deeper, pushing out uncontrollable gasps and moans from my lips. Then I felt him convulse inside me as he pounded into me harder. I gasped in pleasure as I reach the brink of ecstasy.

"Brandon, I'm coming," I screamed.

"Look at me," Brandon commanded. I obeyed and looked into his intense eyes. "Come for me, baby. I want to see you come for me." With that, he plunged deep into me one final time, pushing me off the cliff and I fell deep into the abyss of ecstasy with him.

# CHAPTER FOUR

## *Brandon*

For some reason, I couldn't sleep. I felt relieved that everything was okay with Emma and me. I wasn't sure what I would have done if Des ruined our relationship. I wasn't sure if I would have been able to forgive her. I still couldn't understand why she told Emma she was my girlfriend. Our relationship ended long ago, long before we broke up. During those last few years together, we rarely saw each other and had a relationship centered around our phones.

I had loved her, and she knew that. But I wasn't the same person I was those many years ago—I wasn't the man she fell in love with. I would not allow Des to meddle in my life when

Emma was concerned. I needed to make her understand that. Tomorrow. I'll make sure of it tomorrow.

I let out a deep sigh. A chill ran down my back as the cool night's breeze blew through the open bay window next to Emma's bed. I pulled the down comforter tighter around us as I pulled her closer to me. I listened to her sleeping in my arms and I instantly felt at peace. My fingers gently traced the contours of her body—along her neckline, across her shoulders, and down her arms—leaving a trail of goose bumps behind.

I pulled her closer into me, and like a puzzle piece, her naked body fit perfectly against mine. I kissed the back of her head and inhaled the light floral scent of her hair. She stirred gently and murmured something I couldn't make out. She let out a whimper and then a sigh of pleasure. I wondered if she was dreaming about me. I smiled to myself and hoped she was.

As if in response to my thoughts, I felt her back press deeper against my chest while the curves of her hip and bottom rubbed up against my manhood, instantly igniting a reaction inside of me. I felt my hips involuntarily grind up against her ass as my hardness grew. I wanted to feel the delicious pleasure of being deep inside of her. I wanted to hear her gasp and scream out my name and beg me for more. I wanted to see the carnal pleasure flash in her eyes as she came crashing into ecstasy. When it came to Emma, my desire for her was insatiable—it was a thirst I couldn't quench.

But I resisted the urge to wake her to satisfy my growing need. I had made her come three times tonight, and I knew she was tired. I could wait.

Somewhere between sleep and consciousness, I whispered in her ears, "I'm no longer falling for you, Emma. I'm *in* love with you. You are the woman of my dreams." And with that love drunk feeling swirling inside me, I finally fell asleep with Emma in my arms.

*** 

"Hey, Brandon! Over here," said the familiar voice that I knew belonged to Desiree.

I looked around the bustling coffee shop and saw her smiling brightly, waving her arms at me. I gave a half smile and walked over to her. "Hi, Des. Did you order yet?"

She gave me an enthusiastic hug. "No, I was waiting on you, silly." She grinned and circled her arms around my arm and led me towards the counter where the barista was taking a man's order.

I gently removed my arm from her hold and looked at her. "Des, why did you want to grab breakfast?"

"Well, good morning to you too, Brandon," she said as she crossed her arms and pouted her lips. "Can't I asked a good friend to grab some breakfast before I head back to LA?"

I sighed. "Seriously, Des. What is it? You said on the phone last night that you had some exciting news."

"Well I do. Let's get our coffee first." She smiled at me and looked at me in that way I used to love, a look that came with it an unspoken message of love and desire. It was a look I now dreaded to see on her face. I knew she still had feelings for me. I knew she wanted more. But I didn't feel the same anymore, and I wasn't sure how many times I could tell her that before she believed me.

"Des—" I began.

"I'll have a small decaf Caffé Americano with skim milk please and a chocolate croissant," she said brightly to the barista, cutting me off.

I shook my head and turned to the barista, "Just a large coffee." I pulled out my credit card and handed it to the barista.

Des smiled up at me, "Thanks, hun. You're always such a gentleman."

I rolled my eyes as we moved over to the end of the counter to collect our drinks.

"Des, I have a busy day at work, so I can't stay long," I lied. "Can you please tell me what's going on?" I asked as we sat down at a small corner table.

"Jeez, you're such a buzzkill. Fine." Her expression changed and became more serious. "Well, I didn't just come to SF this past weekend to visit some family like I told you Saturday. I needed to tell you something." She sounded hesitant.

"How come you didn't say anything on Saturday?"

She thought about it for a second before responding. "Well, with that whole thing with Emma running off, I didn't want to bring it up."

"Okay, so what is it that you need to tell me?" I felt anxiety ripple through me. "Is everything okay?"

"Yes, it's … it's okay. It's nothing bad really. It's about us."

"I'm not following, Des." I sighed. "We've had this discussion before. There isn't an 'us' anymore. I'm not sure how to make that more clear to you. We broke up years ago."

"Well that didn't stop us from—"

"Stop it, Des. Let's not go there. I really don't have time to play 20 Questions right now. I'm already late for work. Do you really need to tell me something?" Frustration tapped against my patience, and I waited for her answer.

"Brandon, this is *not* a conversation I want to have when I'm rushed," she said defiantly.

"Des, please listen. We can't keep doing this *every* time we see each other. I can't be your friend if you act like this, especially now that I'm in a relationship. I don't want to hurt you, but I need you to start listening to me. I'm with Emma. I want to be *with* Emma." For a brief moment, I saw the pain in Des's eyes and I wondered if I was too harsh on her.

"Well maybe you'll change your mind after you hear what I have to say." There was something in Desiree's voice that made me uneasy.

"Then tell me. What is it that you need to say to me?" I looked at my watch. I was tempted to just leave the coffee shop now, but guilt kept me rooted in my chair.

"Brandon, this is not easy to say ..." She looked down at her coffee and avoided my eyes.

I felt my impatience grow, and as I got up and began to say, "Okay, I'm going to get going," she said, "Brandon, I'm pregnant."

I felt myself fall back onto my chair as shock paralyzed me. The room seemed to close in on me as I struggled to breathe. "You—you're what? Pregnant?" I looked at her in disbelief.

She nodded, but said nothing.

My mind raced. I had so many questions, but couldn't seem to say them out loud, as if asking them aloud would make them come true.

Several minutes must have gone by when I finally said, "Is it mine?"

Des looked affronted. "Of course it's yours," she hissed. "How could you even ask that?"

"But—but it was just that one time," I stammered, trying desperately to think clearly.

"Well, it only takes that one time. Plus, we were both too drunk to use a condom."

She was right. I was so drunk that night, I had blacked out. I couldn't remember using a condom. "Don't take this the wrong way, but are you sure it's mine?"

"Fuck you, Brandon! Of course it's yours. I haven't been with anyone else. You know I'm not that kind of girl. And actually," she paused and blushed, "I haven't been with anyone else all year."

I opened my mouth, ready to tell her that I needed to be sure, but I stopped myself. I knew she was right. I've known Des for over 11 years, and she may have been a lot of things, but she wasn't someone who slept around. In fact, since we've broken up, I wished she would get out there and start dating—and sleeping around. I wished she would somehow move forward with her life.

"I'm sorry. I shouldn't have said that. So, what … what are you planning to do?"

"What *I'm* planning on doing? You mean what *we're* planning on doing. Brandon, this isn't just my child. And in case you're even considering it, I'm not having an abortion," she said hotly, her voice was now loud enough for the neighboring tables to hear her. I knew she did that on purpose. She wanted others to hear this part of the conversation. But I didn't care. I didn't care what these strangers thought about me.

I was at a loss for words as I tried to process all this. *Des was pregnant. I'm going to be a father. How could this have happened?* I closed my eyes in agony as dread hit me like a ton of bricks as my thoughts went to the one person I truly cared about, the one person I swore I would never hurt again—Emma.

## CHAPTER FIVE

*Desiree*

I watched the agony and fear flash through his eyes, and a part of me felt guilty for breaking this news on him. But I needed to do this. I loved him, and I knew he loved me, even if he didn't think he did.

I looked over at him. He looked pale and in shock, and I wondered what he was thinking. *Was he thinking about her?* I felt a stab of jealousy and felt sick to my stomach. I could not bear the idea that I lost the love of my life to that girl. I pushed the thought of them together out of my mind.

I touched the tiny bump on my stomach beneath my dress and I smiled to myself as my thoughts went to Brandon. I pictured our future together, the future I had always imaged for us, the future we have always talked about since we were 16. This was the right thing to do. I just knew it.

"Brandon?" I asked tentatively. I knew I needed to tread lightly.

He looked up from his thoughts. His eyes were filled with a mixture of emotions. He took a sharp intake of breath and shifted in his chair. "Des, I'm not sure what to say right now. I think I need time to digest all this."

"Will you be there for me at least?" I kept my voice soft.

"Of course, Des. I'll be there for you and the baby. I'll own up to my responsibilities here. I'm just in shock right now and need to figure out what this all means." I could hear the panic in his voice and my heart went out to him.

"Do you want to hear about my plans?" I smiled at him.

"Plans?" He looked confused. "I thought you just said you're keeping it."

"Yes, I am. I meant my plans generally. Since I have family here in SF and you're here …" I paused and looked into his warm, brown eyes—those eyes that I feel in love with so many years ago. "Well, I decided that I'm going to move back to SF. Los Angeles is not a great place to raise a child, and I want the child to be close to you and my family," I paused before I continued, "Will you help me move?" I braced myself for his answer. After so many years with him in my life, I knew Brandon better than I knew myself. I was pretty sure of his answer, but the anticipation still made me uneasy.

"Moving back?" I could hear the terror in his voice. "When?"

"Next week," I said softly.

"When did you decide all this?" His eyes were wild with confusion and shock.

"Actually, just this weekend. After talking to my family about it, I decided that it was the right decision, and I wanted to move now when I'm still able to. Plus, one of my friends just closed on a condo, so she's going to sign over the lease to her apartment to me."

"Next week?" He asked again, as if he didn't hear me correctly when I said it.

I nodded. "Brandon, will you really be there for me and the baby?"

"Yes, of course." There was a sadness in his eyes that I didn't understand.

"I love you, Brandon. I really do." There were tears in my eyes. I was not going to give up on us. I knew that there was something here.

He looked at me, and I saw the pained look on his face that I never liked to see—the look he had when he needed to give someone some bad news. "Des … believe me when I say that I will be there for you and the baby." He paused. "But, that's it. This doesn't change anything between us. I'm with Emma. I love *Emma*."

I cringed. Her name out of his mouth was like nails on a chalkboard for me. His words felt like a cold dagger to my heart. I looked away from him, but kept my face free of emotions. "You may think that now, but I know you love me, Brandon."

He sighed. "Des, I care about you and I do love you, but as a *friend*." His last word was like a hard slap to my face.

"You don't have to admit it, Brandon, but I know how you feel. You wouldn't have made love to me just four months ago if you didn't feel something for me. That's just not you."

"Des, that night was a mistake." I could hear the anger in his voice, which made me flinch. He noticed my pained reaction and his expression softened. "I'm sorry," he said, "I don't want hurt you. But I also don't want to lead you on. We shouldn't have had sex that night. You had just lost your father, and I was there trying to comfort you. I knew you were vulnerable. I shouldn't have let you convince me to take so many shots with you that night. I knew you were trying to numb out the pain. And watching you go through that pain brought back the old painful memories of when I lost my mom, and when you were there for me. In a way, I was trying to numb out my own pain."

He lowered his face and rubbed his temples with his hand and sighed. "I know that's not an excuse for what we did. It's my fault. We shouldn't have slept together."

"It's no one's fault." My voice was strained as I reached over to touch his free hand and squeezed it. "You didn't take advantage of me. I wanted you to make love to me that night," I admitted.

He moved his hand away from me and looked at me. "I'm sorry for hurting you. You don't deserve that, especially not from me. I wish I could give you what you want, but I can't. I just don't have those feelings for you anymore. I'm sorry."

"Okay," I pulled my hand back onto my lap and looked away from him. I knew he remembered the night when he told me he loved me, when he told me he would never love another woman the way he loved me. We just needed some time to reconnect, to rekindle the love we had. He needed to be reminded of how much he had loved me. I would be patient. I would wait until he came around.

## CHAPTER SIX
### *Emma*

I looked at the time on my cell phone and wondered where Brandon was. He was 30 minutes late.

It was Wednesday night before Thanksgiving, and Brandon and I have dinner plans. Tomorrow I was driving north to Sacramento to have Thanksgiving with my mom. The girls were driving into SF Saturday afternoon and staying until Sunday morning. I was really excited to see them. I wish they could stay longer, but Steph and Glo had flights to catch Sunday.

I also really wished that Brandon would be around to meet them too, but he said he had some last minute family thing he had to help out with in Sausalito, a small waterfront town just north of SF, and wouldn't be around all weekend.

My phone beeped. It was Brandon. "Hey, where are you?" I asked.

"Sorry, I got held up. I'm around the corner from your place. Meet me out front in a minute."

"Okay." I grabbed my purse and headed out the door. I was excited to see Brandon. It had been a whole week since we made up, but we haven't spent too much time together. The new projects at work had kept me busy, and when I was free, Brandon seemed to be busy with his projects.

I didn't want to believe it, but sometimes I felt like something was bothering him, like he was preoccupied and always deep in thought in his own world.

I opened the door to Brandon's black Audi S7 and got in. Brandon leaned over and gave me a hug. "Hi babe. Sorry for being late." I inhaled the intoxicating smell of his cologne and felt myself melt into his arms.

"It's okay, but I'm starving. Are we going to make our dinner reservations?"

"Probably," he said, "but I was thinking we can just do something casual, like walk around Fisherman's Wharf and get some clam chowder at one of the vendor at Pier 39. I know it's a bit touristy, but I'd like some fresh air. Is that okay?"

"Sure. I actually haven't been to Fisherman's Wharf since I've moved here, so I'm game," I said cheerfully. I looked at him and felt like something was wrong. "Is everything okay?"

"Yeah. Why do you ask?" He looked at me with concern. He looked tired and stressed, which worried me.

"I don't know. You've just been a little distant since last Wednesday, and I'm not sure why."

"Oh, sorry. I've just been really busy," he said, and immediately added, "With work." He turned away from my gaze and started the engine.

"Are you sure?"

"Yes. Don't worry, Emma. There's nothing wrong." He gave me a quick glance of reassurance before returning to the road. "So I'm sorry again for not being around to meet your friends this weekend. I hope they won't be too upset with me."

I looked at him, trying to study the expression on his face and wondering if he was just tired from work, or whether it was something else.

"It's okay." I felt like I was saying that a lot lately. "I told them that something came up with your family." I don't know why, but I had a feeling there was something more to the story that he wasn't telling me."

"Well I'm glad I can at least house you guys for the weekend. I'm glad my absence was at least useful." He gave me a faint smile, and I tried to return it. Since Brandon would be away all weekend, he offered up his place for the girls to stay during their visit.

"Thanks for offering again. I know we'll be more comfortable there than mine. No one will have to draw straws to see who gets the floor," I joked.

He gave me a smile and turned back to the road.

"So what are your plans for the weekend?" I asked, hoping to get some comfort from his answer.

He remained silent for a few seconds, and then he turned to me with a look of confusion, "Sorry, did you just ask me something?"

"I ... I was just wondering what you were doing this weekend?" *Something was wrong. I just knew it. His heart's not really in this conversation.*

"Oh, I'm just helping out a family member."

"What's wrong? Are they okay?" *Please tell me something.*

"No, nothing like that. Just some last minute family crisis, and I promised I would be around to help out."

"Oh." I didn't hide the disappointment and confusion in my voice as I looked out my passenger side window.

Brandon pulled the car over, stopped the engine, and turned to me. "I'm sorry, Emma."

"Sorry for what?" I prompted.

"I know it feels like things have been strained between us lately. I'm sorry I've been a little preoccupied with some other things."

"So something is going on?" So I was right.

"Yes," I said tentatively, "But it has nothing to do with us, and you have nothing to worry about."

"Oh. What is it? Are you okay?" I asked, trying to get him to tell me more.

"It's nothing you have to worry about. I promise I'll tell you when I know for sure."

His cryptic words confused me, and left me with more questions than answers. "But what—"

"—please, Emma," he interrupted. "Can we just enjoy our night together?"

"Sure." I gave him a small smile, but I was crying and I was screaming at him inside. Something was wrong in Brandon's life and he was shutting me out.

## CHAPTER SEVEN

*Brandon*

After dinner, we took a walk down the pier. The dark, ominous sky stretched across the distant horizon, and a bitter evening breeze blew in from the bay. I put my arm around Emma to keep her warm, but she shrugged it off.

I saw the hurt in Emma's eyes, and my stomach twisted with unease. I held her hand, yet it was limp in my grasp. She had been distant at dinner, deep in her thoughts. Guilt consumed me as the air between us became more tense and uncomfortable. I wanted to make things better, but I just couldn't. I knew she was upset with me, and I hated myself for that.

I wanted and needed to tell her about Des and the pregnancy, but I wasn't ready for that. At least not until after this weekend. This weekend, I wasn't going to be in Sausalito with the family. Instead, I was flying to Los Angeles to help Des move. I promised Des that I would be there for her and our unborn child, and I couldn't back out of that promise.

That was the only lie I've told Emma. Everything else had been true. Des's pregnancy would not affect my relationship with Emma—I would not let it. Even though I was going to have a child with Des, Emma was who I wanted to be with. Emma was who I saw in my future.

"Brandon," she finally said, her voice shaky. "What is going on between us?"

I stopped and pulled her towards me. She avoided my gaze and I knew she was in tears. I held her face with my hands and tilted her face up to look at me. My stomach twisted in agony when I saw the pain in her eyes and my thumb brushed away a tear that was rolling down her cheek.

"Emma, please don't be sad. There's *nothing* wrong between us. Something just came up recently that I need to deal with this weekend. I can't really talk about it right now, but I promise to tell you all about it next week. Okay?"

She nodded, and I felt her body relax a little in my arms. There was a mixture of hope and fear in her eyes. "You promise?"

"Yes. I promise. But again, you have nothing to worry about. *Nothing* will change the way I feel about you."

I lowered my lips onto hers and kissed her tenderly. "You must know how I feel about you, right?"

"I think so," she whispered and I heard the doubt in her voice.

I gazed deeply in her eyes and instantly felt the undeniable connection between us, "Well, in case there is any doubt: I love you, Emma. Nothing has and nothing will change that."

***

"The Chinese food is here," I heard Des's voice from the living room.

"Great. I'm starving," I replied as I taped up the last box of clothes in her bedroom. It was 8:15 p.m. on Saturday and I have spent the last two days helping Des pack up her things into boxes and moving them into the U-Haul truck.

I had agreed to drive the U-Haul to San Francisco for her. I knew Des was an awful driver and I didn't trust her behind the wheel of a large U-Haul truck with our child, especially not a six to seven-hour drive from Los Angeles to San Francisco.

I walked into the living room and a delicious waft of smells hit my nostrils. Des was moving the contents from paper bags. "General Tso's chicken, that's mine. Beef and broccoli, that's yours. And the chow mein and fried egg rolls to share."

I grabbed one of the egg rolls and scoped some of the chow mein and beef and broccoli onto a paper plate. "Well the bedroom is done. Looks like we won't have too much stuff to do in the morning before we take off."

"That's awesome. Thanks for being here." Des smiled at me and handed me a cold bottle of Corona, "Here's a beer."

"I wasn't planning on drinking." *That's what got us into this mess to begin with*, I thought.

"God, Brandon. Live a little," she said as she rolled her eyes. "It's just a beer. I have a couple of leftovers in the fridge, and well, as we both know, I can't drink now, so I need someone to finish them off for me. Don't tell me you're okay with wasting beer?"

"Sorry. Thanks," I said as I took the beer from Des. My eyes darted to the growing bump on her stomach, and a bolt of fear and excitement shot through me. Competing thoughts crossed my mind: *I'm going to be a father. How will Emma react to the news? Will I be ready for all this?*

"Stop staring at me like that." Des's voice broke through my thoughts. I blinked and looked up at her.

"What?"

"You were staring at my stomach like you were in a trance. It's creeping me out." I can tell from her voice that she was more amused than serious.

"Sorry, I just spaced out for a second there." Then a thought came to me. "Hey, how come you didn't tell me sooner about you being pregnant?"

Her expression stiffened and a few seconds passed before she responded, "Well, things were a little awkward after we slept together. I could tell you were avoiding me, so I wanted to give you some space. I wasn't sure until I took a pregnancy test two months later, in September. After that, I was still trying to decide whether I wanted to keep it, to even tell you." She avoided my eye contact, and I wasn't sure if she was crying.

"What made you decide that you wanted to keep it?"

"Because it was your child—*our* child. I would never intentionally destroy a part of you that's inside me."

"Oh." I grappled with the meaning behind Des's words. "Des, I'm ... I'm sorry. I wish I could give you what you want and what you deserve ..." My words trailed off.

"You can," she whispered. My heart ached for her because we both knew that it wasn't true.

About an hour later, I had finished off most of my beef and broccoli, half of the chow mien, and three beers. We ate mostly in silence as I checked and responded to some work emails. I felt myself relax a little from the beers as my muscles began to ache from the long day of heavy-lifting. I stretched and rubbed my neck with my arms.

"Do you need a back massage over there?" Des asked from a few feet away.

"Come on, Des. I'm here to help you move. Nothing else. We've gone over this already. Don't push your luck." I knew I needed to make it clear to Des where I stood with her. I needed there to be no doubt in her mind.

"Alright, alright," she said with her arms in the air. "I was just joking. You used to have a sense of humor, Brandon. What happened to you?"

"Sorry, Des. I just have a lot of on my mind. I know we both made the mistake that night when we slept together. I shouldn't take it out on you."

"Brandon, it wasn't a mistake for me." I heard the hurt in her voice.

"I know, I'm sorry. I didn't mean it that way."

I heard her sigh as she rubbed her tired eyes with her hand. "I'm tired, Brandon. I'm going to go take a shower and get ready for bed."

As she walked away, I was filled with guilt at my harsh words. I knew that I was more at fault than Des was.

I thought back to July when everything happened. Des had called me in the middle of the night in hysterics. She told me that her father had suffered a cardiac arrest earlier that week. They had rushed him to the ER, but attempts to resuscitate him had failed, and he had died en route to the ER. When she called, it was the night of her father's funeral. She was really drunk and was talking irrationally about the meaning of life. Worried that she would hurt herself, I went out and found her roaming around on the beach by herself and brought her back to my place. When we got to my place, she wanted more alcohol and threatened to leave or scream if I didn't give her some. She said she needed to numb the pain. It was a feeling that hit close to home. I had offered her some beer, hoping to keep her calm. The rest of the night was a blur, and the next thing I remembered was waking up with her naked in my arms in my bed.

Just then, my phone went off. It was Emma, and I instantly smiled at the sight of her name.

"Hey babe, how's it going? Shouldn't you be out?" I asked.

"Hiiii ba-by," came Emma's slurred voice from the other end of the line. I could hear loud music and people on her end of the line.

"Emma? Are you drunk? Is everything alright?"

"Nooooo," she said, dragging out the word.

"You're not alright?" I asked, a feeling a cold panic wash through me.

"No silly, I'm aaaaa-okay. I'm just here. With the girls." I heard her giggle uncontrollably.

My body relaxed at her words. "That's great, babe. Are you guys having fun?"

"Hey," she said brightly.

"Yes, I'm here."

"Hey," she said again.

"Can you hear me?"

"Hear what? Hey. Hey. So I want to tell you something."

"Tell him about the hot guy," I heard a distant female voice say.

"Who was that?" I asked. *What guy?* "Where are you guys?" I demanded.

"So I was going to tell you something," she slurred, ignoring my questions.

"Okay, what is it?" I decided to play along.

"Hmm. I forgot." She started giggling again. "Oh wait! I 'member now … so, shhh, don't tell anyone, okay? Promise."

"Um, okay," I agreed tentatively.

"So I think I am a lightweight." There were more giggles.

I laughed. "Emma, are you guys okay? Where are you guys?"

"Umm, I'm not sure. Let me ask Damian," she murmured into the phone.

"Who is Damian?"

"He's ... Hey, Damian, where are we?"

"Hey you. You're at Doc's Clock, sweetie," I heard a male voice yell through the music and noise.

"Oh right. Baby, we're at Doc's Clock."

"Who is this Damian guy?"

"Oh him? Just someone we met tonight. He seems nice," she giggled. "Anyway, I called because I missed you. I'm mad that you're not here."

I chuckled, "I'm sorry, babe. I really wish I was there too. I miss—"

"Hey Brandon, did you need to shower?" came Des's voice from behind me. I quickly moved away from Des, hoping Emma was too drunk to hear that.

"Who was that?" Emma demanded.

My heart leaped out my chest at her words. She wasn't as drunk as I thought. "Who's what?" I asked back, hoping to throw her off. *Shit, why do I keep digging a deeper hole for myself?*

"I thought I heard someone say something. I thought I heard a girl."

"No, there's no girl. That was just the … the TV," I said and attempted a chuckle.

"Really? It just sounded so real, and I thought I heard her say your name," I could hear the doubt in her voice.

"No, I'm just hanging out with the family here, watching TV. It's kind of noisy on your end though, so maybe there's something with our connection. Anyway I should get going. I'm glad you're having so much fun."

"Oh, ok." Her voice was laced with disappointment.

"I can't wait to see you. I miss you."

"Okay, I miss you too. Call me when you're back, okay?"

"I will." I quickly hung up the phone, and looked up to see Des smirking at me and shaking her head.

"I see you didn't tell her everything." There was a satisfaction in her voice that gnawed at my guilt. It was one thing to know I lied to Emma, but quite another to lie to Emma and have Des of all people know about it.

"I'll tell her everything when I see her," I said, reassuring Des as much as I was reassuring myself.

"Well, you better." Her voice was threatening. "Because if you don't, I will."

## CHAPTER EIGHT

*Emma*

"Everything okay?" asked Damian as he handed me another drink. "On the house. You look like you need it."

"Yeah," I finally said. Brief clear thoughts broke through my drunken fog. *I swear I heard a girl's voice.* Even though I knew I shouldn't, I wanted to dial Brandon's number again. I don't know what I would say, but a strong urge to dial his number took over me.

Just as I was about to call him, Steph came rushing to the bar, her face flushed and glowed with alcohol-induced euphoria.

"Shit, how many shots did we have at dinner?" she laughed. "Oh, you're up next on shuffleboard." She had a wide smile on her face as she gave Damian a wink. Then she saw my phone in my hand and frowned. "Did you just call Lover Boy?"

I nodded, feeling guilty. "I know I know. It's girls' night out. I shouldn't have."

"You're the worst!" she teased and laughed.

I gave her a weak smile. "What if he's still interested in his ex," I blurted out.

"Jesus, Emma. I need to smack some confidence in you." Steph tossed her long, wavy blonde hair back behind her shoulder as she sipped from her drink. I notice several guys at the bar eyeing her and watching her every move.

"Emma, you're smart, you're hot, and you have an amazing body. Fuck, if I was guy, I'd bang you."

I laughed. "Thanks, Steph."

"Think about it, he chased after you that morning when that bitch showed up. He called and text you, and even went over to your place. If he was really worried about what that whore thought, he wouldn't have done any of that."

"Yeah, that's true." I thought about Steph's reasoning. Brandon called and texted several times after I had ran out. He also came after me.

If Des was really the one he wanted to be with, and she was in town, he wouldn't have wasted him time to go after me.

"The guy obviously gaga about you and wants to be with you, and the bitch knows it. She's just jealous. You're fucking the man she wants."

"Yeah."

"Just remember, she might want him back, but if he loves you, nothing *she* does will change that unless you *let* it." Steph was right. I couldn't let Des win. There was nothing she could say or do that would make me not love Brandon. So long as he wanted me in his life, I was going to stay with him. There was nothing Des could do to change that unless I let it happen. And I know I would not give up Brandon for anything.

"Thanks, Steph. You're totally right. Maybe I should call Brandon to apologize. I was acting kind of weird and suspicious when we ended the call."

"Don't be an idiot. Give me your phone. You're on time out," she said as she grabbed my phone and dropped it in her purse.

"But—" I tried to protest.

"Emma, snap out of it. You really need to learn how to play hard to get," she said as she ordered another drink from Damian.

"It's not like that between us though," I tried to reason, though a part of me was unsure of that now.

"Girl, *every* guy loves a chase. Shit, I love the chase, and last time I checked, I'm not sporting a pair of balls down there," she laughed. "The point is, stop calling him so much. Give him a chance to miss you."

Even in my intoxicated state, I knew Steph was right. "Okay," I resolved. "Maybe you're right."

"I know I'm right," Steph said with an air of confidence.

I laughed. "Okay, I'll try not to call or think about him for the rest of the time you guys are in town."

"Good. And it shouldn't be too hard. There's some nice distractions to help you with that," Steph said as her eyes gestured sideways to Damian, who was approaching them with Steph's drink order.

"Damian, babe, Emma needs a distraction tonight so she doesn't drive herself crazy thinking about her estranged boyfriend. You seem like you'd be great at that sort of thing," she said, flashing Damian her sexiest smile.

Damian leaned across the bar towards us, and as his hands pressed against the edge of bar counter, his biceps flexed, causing the intricate arm-length tattoo down his left arm move as if the designs were alive. "Anything for a pretty face." His voice was husky as he bore his piercing blue eyes into me, sending a jolt of excitement through me. His lips curled in a wicked smile, and I knew he was trouble.

"Thanks. Now I'm going to go check up on Jill and Glo. I'll be right back," Steph gave me a wink and began to walk away.

"Steph," I hissed under my breath, "I'm not interested."

Steph rolled her eyes and whispered back, "Emma, relax. It's just innocent flirting. Something's obviously up with Brandon that's gotten you all on edge. You need to relax and get your mind off of him for the night."

"Steph," I hissed again after her as I watched her walk to across room where Jill and Glo were playing shuffleboard with two guys.

"Don't worry. I don't bite. I can tell you're a good girl," said Damian as he checked out Steph's backside as she walked away.

I rolled my eyes, but something inside me resented his comment, "No, I'm not. I make mistakes," I retorted.

He laughed. "You don't even know what a bad girl is."

"I—" I began to protest, but stopped. He was right.

"You seem like a sweet girl who probably deserves a sweet guy. But, if you ever want to be a bad girl, give me a call." He scribbled his name and number on a thin, paper coaster and handed it to me. "I won't say any 'I love yous,' but I promise you a great time with no strings attached" He licked his lips and winked at me. His piercing, blue eyes illuminated against his dark, bronze complexion. Everything about this guy oozed sex and danger. And a small part of me was turned on by him.

I smiled nervously and accepted the coaster. "Thanks. I, uhm, should go and check up on my friends," I said as I shoved the coaster with his number aimlessly into my purse and quickly walked away from the bar.

I knew he watched me walk away, as he had done with Steph. I could sense his eyes looking me up and down and a shiver ran down my body. A part of me was excited by this man, but I knew that I wasn't the type of girl that could have a night of fun with no strings attached. Damian was right. I had no idea what a bad girl was. I was a nice girl, and right now, all I wanted was to be with Brandon.

***

The air was chilly and I felt light drizzles of rain fall on my cheeks as I entered the lobby of Brandon's building. Nervous energy jolted through me as I waited for the elevator to take me up to his condo on the penthouse floor.

It was Monday and he had invited me over tonight for dinner and "to talk." I was excited to see him, but I also knew this wouldn't be your ordinary dinner date. Whatever he had to tell me, it must have been big. It had been causing a silent rift between us for over a week now—a tension that was almost palpable in the air. That terrified me.

I knew I would be devastated if I lost Brandon. The amount of pain that had hit me with the misunderstanding with Desiree was still fresh in my mind. Whatever this was, I knew it would not be a misunderstanding. It would be real, and it would be much more painful.

I drew in a deep breath, trying to calm myself, and knocked on Brandon's front door.

"Hey you," he smiled at me warmly when he opened the door and pulled me into his embrace. "God I've missed you."

I sunk into him and inhaled his familiar, comforting scent of aftershave and laundry detergent. "I've missed you too." I looked up at him and pulled his face down to mine. Our lips met in a slow passionate kiss that melted away some of my anxiety.

"I've definitely missed that," Brandon whispered when our lips separated. "So how are you? Did you have fun with your friends this past weekend?"

"Yeah, we had a great time. Here's your keys. Thanks again for letting us stay over at your place. It was definitely much more comfortable than my studio."

He chuckled, "I think I should be the one thanking you guys."

I looked at him in confusion.

"I arrived home to a much cleaner place than I had left it. So thanks for cleaning the place. I should invite you over more often." He chuckled as he pulled me into his hard chest.

I laughed. "That's all Jill and her anal-retentiveness. So don't get any ideas. You're not getting a maid out of me."

"Well, that's too bad," he said as we walked through the hallway. "I was hoping I could watch you clean."

There was something in his voice that made me stop and look at him. He grinned at me, and I could see a flash of desire in his eyes. He then pulled me into his arms again, "In the spirit of compromise, will you at least wear a maid's outfit?" he whispered as he gave me a devious smile, and I felt my body tingle with anticipation.

"Compromise? I didn't know we were in negotiations. What's in it for me?" Before he could answer, I pulled him down towards me, and I kissed him eagerly, my arms wrapped tightly around his neck. Our lips moved together with complete abandonment, as if each kiss were the last.

Then, in one fluid moment, he moved me with him and backed me up against the wall, his lips never leaving mine as he hungrily explored my mouth with his tongue. My nails dug into his shirt as he pressed his growing erection against my inner thigh between our clothes. I unzipped my skirt and pushed it down to the ground, needing one less layer of separation between us. His lips left mine as it explored my neck and earlobes.

"Yes, we're negotiating," he panted in my ear, his hot breath sending chills down my back. "Do you really want to know what's in it for you?" he asked seductively.

"Yes," I said breathlessly.

"This is what you would get in exchange." Before I knew what was happening, he was bent down before me, looking up at me. "Spread your legs," he commanded. I obliged. Suddenly, his head was between my legs. "Bend your knees over my shoulders," he ordered and I writhed in anticipation as I did exactly what he asked. He then stood up, lifting me up with him over his shoulders. I could feel his breath against my inner thigh and heard him inhale me in.

"Do you know how crazy you're driving me?" I heard the raw need in his voice, and I instantly felt a wetness flow below as desire coursed through me. I felt his fingers move aside my panties as his tongue plunged inside me, lapping me up as I gasped in agonizing pleasure, overwhelming my every thought. My hands grasped violently at his hair as my body exploded with hot spasms of pleasure as his tongue entered me again and again, until finally, I reached the apex of pleasure before crashing into the depths of ecstasy.

When he lowered me down to the ground, I was still panting, my body was numb and tingled from the afterglow of pleasure. "That was—that was amazing," I stuttered. I pulled him in for a kiss and tasted myself on his tongue.

"So does that mean we have a deal? Maid outfit?" he grinned.

I giggled. "I'm sure we can work something out."

"I'm looking forward to it."

"I haven't made you come yet," I continued as I pushed my hand down inside his jeans.

He threw his head back and groaned in pleasure as my hands found his satiny, hard erection. "God, you have no idea how much I want to fix that problem right now," he gasped. "—but we should eat first before the food gets cold."

As if in agreement, my stomach growled. We both laughed. "Okay, well I'll go get cleaned up," I said as I kissed him lightly on the lips.

I walked towards the hallway leading to the restroom, my body buzzing with euphoria. When I passed the laundry room, an unzipped duffle bag sitting on top of the washer caught my eye.

This hadn't been here yesterday morning when the girls and I were here. Some of the contents of the duffle bag spewed out from it, and it was then that I saw it, sitting on top of some clothes and half hidden from view. My breath caught and my body stiffened as my mind raced frantically, trying to understand what this all meant.

It was a half-opened yellow prism-shaped chocolate bar. It was a Toblerone.

Memories of what Brandon said to me at the airport several weeks ago flooded back to me. We had been waiting for our flight to D.C. for the Imperial Hotel Project, and he had bought a Toblerone. *"I never buy these things normally, but for some reason, I always buy a bar of it when I'm at an airport."*

My heart grew heavy as I realized what this meant. *Brandon was at an airport this past weekend.*

## CHAPTER NINE

### *Brandon*

"Emma? Are you okay in there?" I yelled down the hallway towards the bathroom. Ten minutes must have passed since she went to clean up. *What could be taking her so long?*

When I didn't hear a reply, I walked towards the hallway leading to the bathroom and turned the corridor, and found Emma standing motionless in the hallway in front of the laundry room. Her face was pale and she looked like she saw a ghost.

"Hey, what's wrong? Are you hurt?" I asked as I rushed to her side. I examined her, making sure she wasn't hurt. Then I saw the pain in her eyes and I knew something was definitely wrong. "Emma? Talk to me," I pleaded as I pulled her into my arms and held her tightly against me. Something deep inside my stomach twisted in anxious dread.

She pushed me away with force, "Don't touch me. We both know something is going on that you haven't been telling me," she held out her hand, revealing a Toblerone bar. "You told me once that you only bought these when you were at airports. That bag wasn't here this weekend when the girls and I were staying here."

I followed her gaze and saw the tote bag I had used this weekend in LA.

"You told me that you were in Sausalito this weekend, that's just a few miles north of here. Why were you at an airport?" she asked accusingly.

I looked at her surprise. I had planned on telling her everything tonight after dinner. This was not how I expected her to find out. "Emma, I—"

She cut me off. "When I called you Saturday night, I heard a girl's voice. You said it was the TV, but I didn't believe you then, and I definitely don't believe you now. Who is she?" Her voice shook as it rose in volume.

Dread paralyzed me as I looked at her. Her face twisted with pain as tears gathered in her eyes. A part of me wanted to lie—to tell her that it was all just a misunderstanding, that it was just an old Toblerone bar from a previous trip, and that she was overreacting.

But one look into her eyes, and I knew that it was time to tell her everything. I had to tell her the whole truth now or I may lose her forever.

"Emma, please let me explain." I tried to keep my voice calm. "Can we sit down and talk? I wanted to tell you everything."

"When?" she bellowed as anger entered her voice. "After you fucked me? When, Brandon?"

"Emma, *please*," I begged. "I wanted to tell you tonight. It's not what you think?"

"What I *think* is that you lied to me when you said you were in Sausalito this past weekend. What I *think* is that you lied to me when I asked if you were with a girl Saturday night. Am I wrong?" I heard the anger in her voice, but saw the sadness in her eyes.

"God, Emma. I'm a fucking idiot for not telling you everything sooner. But it's really not what you think. *Please* give me a chance to explain."

Then Emma's expression changed. The anger on her face evaporated, like someone had let out the air out of a balloon. She looked tired, and I hated myself for putting her through this. She finally gave a small nod as she looked away from me.

"Let's sit down." I gestured to the living room, and she led the way with me walking behind her.

I could hear my heart beating violently against my chest. In the last few days, I had imagined how I would tell Emma everything, how she would react, and how I would make her see that things would be okay. I imagined how I would show her that regardless of what happened, I loved her, and I would not stop loving her. But now, now that she was in front of me, now that I saw the look on her face, I wasn't as confident about how things would play out.

We sat down on the couch. I held her hands firmly and I felt them shaking in my grasp. "Emma, I need you to know that I love you. Can you promise me that you'll remember that? None of this changes anything about us or how I feel about you."

She looked at me with a confused and distressed look on her face, like an innocent deer caught in the headlights, awaiting its impending death. My heart twisted as a cold certainty hit the pit of my stomach: I was going to hurt her again.

I squeezed her hands, hoping it would convey all the emotions that I had for her, hoping she would forgive me. Her hands were cold and clammy and motionless. She looked at me without saying a word, waiting for me to explain myself.

"So you're right," I began as I nervously watched her expression as I spoke. "Something has been going on and I haven't been completely honest with you."

She looked wounded by my words, as if she wasn't expecting my admission. A feeling of unease fell over me as I thought about everything I had to tell her.

"Well, uhm, this weekend, I was in Los Angeles," I paused, trying to figure out how to explain everything. My thoughts felt muddled and all I could focus on was the pain on Emma's face, a pained look that I knew would only get worse.

"I was with Desiree." I saw the color drain from Emma's face, and immediately added, "*Nothing* happened. I was just helping her pack and move."

"Help her move?" Emma's voice was soft. "Why? Where is she going? Why does she need your help?"

"She's, uh, she's moving to SF," I admitted. "She wanted to be closer to her family."

"And you," added Emma pointedly.

I knew I couldn't respond to that. I couldn't because it was true, and it was a truth I didn't want to admit to Emma.

Then I saw a spark of understanding in her eyes that quickly turned into anguish. "So the girl's voice I heard Saturday night when I called you, the voice that asked if you needed the shower. That was Des?"

"Yes," I admitted, "but we had just finished moving most of her stuff into the U-Haul. She was just asking if I needed to use the shower. Nothing happened."

There was a pause and I could tell that Emma was deep in thought. "I don't get it," she finally said.

"What do you mean?" I asked.

"Why were you helping her move? Why did you lie about it? And why didn't you tell me sooner?" The questions spewed out of her.

"I did want to tell you. Believe me, I did. I just ... I just didn't know how to tell you."

"Tell me what? What's going on, Brandon?"

"There's ..." I took a deep breath to clear my head, "There's something that happened between Des and I that I haven't told you," I began. "This all happened before we started dating," I quickly added, hoping to reassure her.

"Okay, what is it?" she asked nervously.

"Let me start from the beginning," I paused, "About four months ago, Des's father passed away suddenly from cardiac arrest. She had called me late one night after the funeral. She was really drunk, and possibly suicidal."

A spark of concern hit Emma's face. "She tried to commit suicide?"

"I'm not sure if she would have, but I wasn't about to wait around to find out. She had overdosed on painkillers in the past, shortly after we broke up. Luckily, a friend found her in time and called 911. They had pumped her stomach and were able to remove most of the pills. The doctors had said that if she hadn't gotten to the hospital when she did, her body would have digested most of the pills, and she probably wouldn't have made it."

I saw the shock on Emma's face, and I squeezed her hands. "She's better now."

I paused before continuing, "So when she called that night after her father's funeral, I could tell she was in trouble. I found her drunk and walking around aimlessly alone on the beach. I convinced her to come back to my place with me. I needed to make sure she wouldn't do anything stupid. When we got back here, she wanted to drink more. She convinced me to drink with her—to honor the memory of her father, she said. We had a number of shots …" I trailed off. As Emma listened to my story, I saw the anxiety build in her eyes.

"… the next thing I remember was waking up in bed … with her."

A look of horror painted Emma's face and a part of me didn't want to tell her anything more—to cause her any more pain. But I knew I had to.

"So you know that Des was in town a few weeks ago. Well … she told me that … she's pregnant. And I'm the father." I cringed when I heard the words out loud.

Emma was silent. Her face was pale and expressionless. She avoided my gaze as she sat in front of me in shock.

"When did you know?" she finally said dryly.

"She told me the day after that night I came over for dinner," I said cautiously.

I saw the hurt in her eyes. "That was almost two weeks ago," she accused. "At what point were you going to tell me? After she had the baby?" The anger returning to her voice.

"I really did want to tell you sooner, but I was trying to come to terms with all this myself. I … I should have told you as soon as I found out, but I needed time to think about everything. I wanted to talk to her some more—to be sure she was going to keep the baby before I approached you about this …"

"So she's keeping it?" she whispered.

I nodded solemnly.

I watched Emma's expression and waited for her to respond. But she didn't.

"Emma, I'm really sorry for not telling you sooner. But please know that this does not change anything between us. I love you, and I want to be with *you*. Nothing will change that. Des may be a part of my life, but I'm not going to let that affect us. Please know that."

She remained silent and I could not shake the dread that gripped my heart.

"Emma, please talk to me. What can I do to make things right—to make this work between us. I'll do anything," I pleaded.

"That's just it. There's nothing you *can* do," she whispered flatly, her voice barely audible.

The look in Emma's eyes confirmed my greatest fear—a cold certainty that I had lost her.

# CHAPTER TEN

## *Emma*

I was on the verge of tears as I sat there. As the reality of what Brandon had just told me started to worm its way into me, my past came crashing back to haunt me.

*I can't be with him.*

The room began to close in on me as I thought through everything Brandon had just told me; I felt my life unraveling before me and I couldn't breathe. Suddenly, I sprung to action. I needed to get out of here. Away from Brandon.

"Where are you going?" Brandon asked, grabbing my arm. "Can we please talk about it?"

"There's nothing to talk about, Brandon!" My voice was shrill and shaky. "I can't do this?"

"Do what? Emma, what are you trying to say? Please tell me what you're thinking," he pleaded.

"I'm sorry. I ..." I said. I headed towards the door as he followed behind. I reached for the doorknob and then stopped and turned back to him.

"Actually," my voice stronger than I felt, "I'm not sorry. This is not my fault. I didn't ask for this. You promised you wouldn't hurt me again!"

I ran out the door and towards the elevator. My body was reeling from shock.

"Emma, I'm so sorry! I know I fucked up. I know this mess is entirely my fault, but please don't do this. Please don't just leave like this. I would never hurt you intentionally. What I did with Des, that happened before we started dating. You're the one I want to be with, and none of this has changed that."

"Everything has changed, Brandon," I cried as I entered the elevator. "I can't—" I couldn't believe I was about to say this, "I can't be in a relationship with you. Please let me go."

I saw the shocked expression on his face as the elevator closed between us. Tears began to fall down my face as I found myself yet again in this elevator in tears. I sobbed uncontrollably as the elevator took me down to the lobby.

Pain engulfed me and I found myself spiraling down a darkness that I had tried to escape a long time ago. A darkness that would be forever a part of my past, forever a part of me. I had thought that there was nothing Des could do or say that would make me give Brandon to her. Not when Brandon still loved me.

But I was wrong. So wrong. I hadn't expected my past to be on her side.

***

It was raining heavily when I got outside. Yet, I ran out of the building and into the night, embracing the cold rain that hit my skin. The wind blew through my hair, moving it violently in the air, as if it had a mind of its own.

I ran. Away from him, away from the pain, and away from the reality of what just happened—the reality that Brandon and I could never be. My lungs burned with exhaustion, and my feet ached as my stilettos pounded against the wet pavement.

Then I heard his voice through the downpour of rain. I turned around right as his hand grabbed my arm and pulled me to a stop.

"Emma, stop! I am *not* going to let you run away from me like this. Not again. I will not lose you over this," he shouted.

"You already have, Brandon," I yelled over the rain that pounded down on us. "We can never be together. You're going to be a father. I can not take that away from an unborn child. I just can't."

"Emma, I don't understand. I will be there for the baby, but that doesn't mean we can't be together. That doesn't make sense. Why does it matter?"

"It just does," I cried. I have kept this secret locked away since the day my mom told me years ago. How could I tell anyone now?

"It should not matter, Emma. I love you. I did not cheat on you. I am not with Des. Even if we weren't together, I am not going to date Des. We broke up many years ago for a reason. A baby doesn't change that."

I shook my head violently as I sobbed.

He pulled me into his arms and hugged me tightly. "I'm telling you right now, it will *not* change a thing between us. I love you and I want to be with *you*!"

I pushed Brandon away from me. Being in his arms made things that much more painful. It was a reminder of what I couldn't have.

"But it does change us, Brandon! It changes EVERYTHING! She's won! She had won before I even moved here. Before I was even in the picture. She had won the day you guys slept together and she got pregnant!"

Saying the words aloud made my heart ache. It ached with so much intensity, I thought I was going to die. At this moment, I wanted to die. To no longer feel any of this pain that crushed against my chest.

"Emma, you're shivering and you're completely soaked. Please, let's just go back inside and talk things through." His voice was desperate and pleading.

"I can't, Brandon. We can't be together. There's nothing you can say that will change that," I choked out.

"Why? I don't understand. Do you not love me?"

I looked up at him, surprised that he would even ask that. "Of course I do."

"Then what is it? Why can't we be together? Are you mad at me for what I've done?"

"I am, but that's not it. It has nothing to do with you. It's me. I just can't," I cried. I didn't want him to know the one thing that I was ashamed of.

"No, Emma," he said forcefully. "That's not good enough. I will not let you do this again. I will not allow you to run away and shut me out. You can't tell me you love me and then tell me we can't be together. I know you're upset with me, but what happened between Des and I was before anything really happened between us. You can be mad at me, you can hit me, and you can take it out on me, but you cannot—and I will not let you—hold that mistake against me and what we have. I will not let you break up this relationship because of it." His hands firmly held my arms, preventing me from turning away from him, preventing me from escaping the truth.

"My mom was raped, Brandon!" I screamed. I then gasped at my own admission.

"What?" Brandon's grip on me loosened as he took in my words. "Why are you telling me this? Please, Emma. I don't understand."

My body shook—from the pain, from the grief over my mother, from the hatred over my father, and from the loss of Brandon. I knew there was no turning back now. I had to tell him everything.

"Can we please go back inside to talk about this?"

I shook my head. "I need to tell you now before I change my mind."

"Okay." His worried eyes examined me as he guided me towards an awning in front of a closed shop. "Let's get out of the rain at least."

"She was 19. He was a friend in college. My mom said that she was at a party of his and she had too much to drink. She had passed out at some point, and he raped her when she was unconscious. She never reported it because he said he would deny it. He threatened her. He said it would be a he-said-she-said, and he would smear her name and reputation in town if she said anything. Because he came from a prominent family in town, she knew he had the power to destroy her life and get away with it. I also think that she was ashamed to tell people—like somehow, it was her fault. Anyway, a few months later, my mom found out that she was pregnant."

I paused and looked at Brandon. He was silent as he listened. Then I saw the look of understanding flash in his eyes.

"She kept the baby," he whispered.

I nodded as I avoided his gaze.

"And that baby was you."

"Yes," I said somberly. This was the first time I've ever told anyone about my past—about the deep secret I was ashamed of. "I was the product of a rape," I whispered.

Brandon looked stunned and unable to speak. I could tell he wasn't sure how to react or what to say. I reached for his hands and held them, and he reacted by pulling me into his arms and held me protectively.

"I'm so sorry, Emma."

I felt fresh, hot tears roll down my cheeks as I buried myself his hard chest. He felt warm and safe, and I felt the pang of losing him to Desiree—to the child.

I pulled away to look up at him. Although the shame of my past twisted inside me, a part of me felt a sense of freedom that my secret was out, and that it was Brandon who I told. He gave me a reassuring smile.

"My mom told the guy about being pregnant. He had promised to support us and to be there for me. But by the time I was born, he was in a serious relationship with another woman. He skipped town and denied being my father. My mom was devastated. Not because she love my father, but because she knew that she would need help raising me. And during most of her pregnancy, my father had promised her that money would not be an issue. So she was not prepared financially when I was born. She had to drop out of college to work two jobs to provide for us."

I looked at Brandon. There was no pity on his face, just unadulterated concern and sadness, and I felt my feelings for this man deepen.

"I've never met my father," I continued. "I don't even know his name or what he looks like. I took my mom's maiden name. My mom didn't tell me what happened until I was 13. All my life before that point, I loved a father that I thought had passed away before I was born. When I found out the truth, I *hated* him. I hated him for abandoning my mom and me, I hated him for breaking his promise to support us. I told myself I would never allow someone to do that to another child if I had the power to prevent it."

My voice shook as I told my story, and I wiped the tears from my eyes.

I saw the understanding in Brandon's eyes. "I see. So … you're ending our relationship because you don't want to interfere with the relationship I will have with my child?"

I nodded. "I don't expect you to completely understand my reasoning, but I know what it's like to have a father that didn't love you enough to stay in your life. A father who abandoned you and never looked back. It is devastating. I can't do that to an innocent child."

"But … Emma, you *know* me. I wouldn't do that. I wouldn't abandon a child like that. I'll take responsibility for the child. But that doesn't mean I have to be with Des. I want to be with you."

I sighed. I know what he said made complete sense, but this was something I felt strongly about. "I just can't, Brandon. I swore to myself I would never be the other woman. The woman my father left me for. Yet, here I am. I am *that* woman. I just can't do that. I can't be the other woman."

"Emma, I'm *so* sorry for fucking things up and making such a mess out of everything. I'm sorry for lying about it initially. But I think we can still work through this. I know it's a lot to take in right now. I think you just need some time to think about things. Please just don't give up on us. Please."

I looked into him pleading eyes and my heart broke. I knew I couldn't be with him. I would be becoming the person I hate for so long—the other woman who took my father away from me. I could not do that to an innocent child. I knew it was irrational to think this way, but I thought this way nonetheless.

"I'm sorry, Brandon. I just can't. I need to go now." Sadness overwhelmed me at the thought of letting him go, but I knew that the longer I stayed with him, the harder it would be.

"Emma," he held onto me, his grip firm and unwavering. "I love you. Please know that I have made a lot of mistakes with us, but telling you that I love you was not one of them. Please hold on to that. Just think about it."

I nodded. I didn't mean it, but I couldn't see him hurt anymore. I saw a cab approaching and I raised my arm to hail it down.

"Goodbye, Brandon." I gave him one last hug, holding in all my feelings inside.

"Emma ... please think about it," he whispered in my ear.

I got into the cab without saying another word. I waved a goodbye to him as the car pulled away. He stood there, looking at me in shock.

When he was finally out of sight, I sobbed. I sobbed for everything I just lost. I sobbed for everything I will never have.

\*\*\*

By the time the cab dropped me off at my place, I was drenched and cold. My body felt numb. My emotions were all over the place, and I was not myself. The initial anger I had felt when Brandon told me about everything he was hiding had returned.

*How could he have had sex with Des? Was he lying to me now when he says he has no feelings for her? Could you really stop loving someone after loving them for eight years? After they were there for you? After they pulled you out of the depths of a tragedy? Could you not love someone who is the mother of your child?*

I felt my thoughts spinning out of control. I shook my head violently, trying to stop the thoughts from circling in my mind. "Does it even matter? I can never be with him. Does it even fucking matter?" I cried out loud. I was filled with rage at this point. I was angry at Brandon, angry at Des, and angry at my father.

In frustration, I threw my purse across the room; it hit against the edge of the coffee table and the contents spewed out onto the floor.

Of the contents, a thin piece of paper caught my attention—the thin paper coaster with Damian's number on it.

Without thinking, I ran over and picked up the coaster. I didn't know why, but at this moment, I felt reckless. I felt irrational. A part of me wanted to hurt Brandon the way he had hurt me. The other part of me just wanted all the pain to go away, no matter the consequences. All signed pointed to Damian.

I dialed the number and Damian picked up after the third ring.

"Hello?" came a husky voice.

"Hi. Is this Damian?"

"The one and only. Who's this?"

"It's Emma. I was at your bar on Saturday night. You gave me your number."

"Oh yeah, I remember you. The hot blonde with the boyfriend issue."

"There's no boyfriend," I said flatly.

"Oh," there was a pause. "Sorry. So why are you calling?"

"I can't be alone right now. I was wondering—Can I come over now? I need a distraction," I heard myself blurt out.

"Sounds like you've had a rough day. Sure, come over."

I scribbled down his address. Then I took a quick shower, threw on a nice top and jeans, and applied some makeup to mask the puffiness that was developing around my eyes. I knew that this wasn't like me. The normal Emma wouldn't call some random guy and go over to his place in the middle of the night. But tonight, I didn't care. The last thing I wanted to be, was me.

I looked at myself in the mirror, and felt a pang of guilt. "You *need* to let him go. You *need* a distraction right now. You *need* someone to help ease this pain," I tried to reassure myself.

***

Fifteen minutes later, I found myself standing at the front door of Damian's place in the Mission District. My heart was pounding and I was nervous. My heartache was temporarily replaced with a thrill I never felt before.

The door opened, and there stood Damian—shirtless, and flashing me his signature, wicked smile. My eyes immediately focused on the elaborate dragon tattoo across his chest.

"Hey gorgeous." He pulled me into him—pressing me against his hard, bronze chest—and gave me a kiss on the cheek.

"Hi," I said breathlessly. *I need this distraction*, I reminded myself.

"So what's up? Want a drink?" he said as he headed to the kitchen.

"God, yes," I said.

"What's your poison?"

"Whatever's strong enough to numb out the pain," I blurted out.

He laughed. "That bad, eh?"

I knew coming here wasn't a good idea, but tonight, I didn't care. I spent my entire life playing it safe, waiting for *the one* to give my all to, and where did that get me? Nowhere. All I got in return was a lot of heartache.

"Here you go," he said handing me shot.

"What is it?" I asked as he held out his own shot.

"It's my version of an I.V.—Italian Valium. It's got Amaretto and Bacardi 151 instead of the normal Amaretto and gin mix," he explained.

"Oh."

"You said you wanted it strong," he said with a smirk. "That will get you where you want to go—a place without pain."

"Thanks." I raised my shot glass towards his, "To bad choices," I said.

He laughed. "I'll drink to that."

I downed my shot and winced as the alcohol burned its way down my throat. "Can you make me another one?" I said as I put down my shot glass.

Damian looked at me in amusement, "You're not one to take things slow, are you?"

"Not tonight," I challenged, feeling the liquor courage course through my veins.

Damian made us another round of I.V. shots.

"To a numbing existence," I said as I downed the second shot, which went down a little easier than the first.

"Another," I demanded.

"Here, I'll make you a mix drink, and we can just hang."

*What are you doing here?* a tiny voice said inside my head. "Um. No. Thanks, Damian. I shouldn't be here. I should get going."

"Oh? Do you have somewhere to go?" he asked, giving me a sidelong glance.

His question was like salt on a fresh wound. "No … no, actually. I don't," I said defiantly.

"So stay." He gave me a look that both excited and scared me. *You're playing with fire*, the tiny voice warned me. I didn't have to know this man long to know that he was reckless, wild, and carefree. Normally, he would be the type of guy I would stay far away from. He was trouble.

But at this moment, that was exactly what I wanted—what I needed.

"Okay, I'll stay."

"So, tough day?" he asked as he fixed me a mixed drink.

"You can say that. I don't really want to talk about it though." I walked over to his couch. I was starting to feel the effects of the alcohol and needed to sit down.

"Here you go." Damian handed me my drink and sat down next to me on the couch. I felt his shorts rub against my thigh and felt a spark of excitement at the contact.

He turned his body towards me and looked at me. My eyes darted between his intense, blue eyes and his hard muscular chest. I flushed when I saw him catching me admiring his body.

"Blushing is a sign of a good girl," Damian teased.

"No, I'm not blushing," I said defensively. "It's just the alcohol."

"Ahh, right." He was unconvinced. "So, what made you decide to call me?"

"I ... I needed a distraction." I realized how offensive that may have sounded, and said, "Sorry, I didn't mean it that way. I just ..."

He laughed. "No need to explain. I get it. You're looking for a fun time." He gave me a sinful smile and reached over and brushed his finger along my jawline, sending goose bumps down my arms. "And I'm *a lot* of fun."

"Are you going to kiss me?" I heard myself ask out loud. I then cringed at how stupid I must have sounded.

He leaned towards me and whispered in my ear, "Well that's up to you." He lingered near my face and I could feel his hot breath against my ear and down my neck. "What would you like to do?"

"I …" my voice trailed off. A small part of me wanted to kiss him, wanted to think about something else besides Brandon.

He didn't wait for me to decide. Before I could register what was happening, his lips were on mine, sucking and tasting my lips and tongue like an expert.

I heard myself left out a moan, and a wave of guilt washed over me. I quickly pushed it away—I'm here to *not* think about Brandon. With that thought, I pulled Damian closer towards me and kissed him back with force and desperation. I thought maybe, just maybe, the more contact I felt from Damian, the less I would be tormented by thoughts of Brandon.

Damian responded as only he could. In one swift movement, he was on top of me and laid my back onto the couch. He anchored himself on top of me with one hand as his mouth continued to explore mine, the other hand glided its way under my shirt and effortlessly unhooked my bra strap. Within seconds, his rough hands cupped and kneaded my breast. Then all my clothes were off and on the floor.

"Fuck, your body is amazing," he growled as he admired me with lust-filled eyes. "The things I can do to you."

Nerves started to worked their way through my drunken stupor as I saw him take off his shorts, revealing his long and hard erection.

The second his naked body was on top of mine, I knew everything was all wrong. I knew I didn't want to do this—no matter how much I was upset with Brandon, no matter how much pain I wanted to escape from. This just wasn't me.

"Stop!" I cried.

"What the fuck?" Damian jumped off of me, confused at what just happened.

"I ... I can't do this. I—" I wasn't sure what to say.

Damian laughed and shook his head, "You're a fucking tease, you know that? A *hot* fucking tease."

I looked at him in disbelief. "Why are you laughing? You're not upset?"

"Well, I'm not going to lie and say I didn't want to fuck you tonight. But, no. I'm not upset. Like I said at the bar the other night, you're not a bad girl. You're just going through some shit."

"I'm sorry, Damian." I broke into a sob as I thought about everything that had happened earlier tonight.

"Hey, hey. This apartment is a no-cry zone. Don't cry. We don't have to have sex," he teased. "Honestly, I'm surprise you've gone this far."

"Oh." I looked at him in surprise. "Damian, you're actually a nice guy."

He laughed. "Don't be fooled. I'm not a nice guy. But I'm also not a guy who will force someone to do something they don't want to do. I'll rock your world if you want me to. But if you don't want the best sex of your life, no hard feelings. There's plenty of girls who will."

I giggled, and then sighed. "Thanks for cheering me up."

"No problem. So what do you want to do then?" He gave me a wicked smile.

"Well, first, I should put on my clothes," I said as I picked up my clothes from the floor.

"That's unfortunate," he teased.

"Do you mind if I sleep—just sleep—with you tonight? I just don't want to be alone," I admitted.

"Not a problem. Hey, I'll be right back," he said as he got up from the couch.

"Where are you going?"

"Bathroom to jack off," he said matter-of-factly. Then he looked at me and then at his erection. "This shit doesn't go down on its own, so if we're not having sex tonight, I'll have to put it to bed." He laughed at his joke.

"Oh," I said.

My eyes followed his gaze and saw his rock, hard erection and quickly looked away. My face was hot with embarrassment.

He laughed. "Again, good girl," he said as he pointed a finger at me.

I stared in shock after him as he walked completely naked towards the backroom.

He laughed when he noticed the shocked look on my face. "What can I say? I'm what you'd call a man-whore." With that, he closed the bathroom door behind him and jacked off.

# CHAPTER ELEVEN

## *Brandon*

A few weeks have passed since the night Emma told me about her secret. It was the last thing I had expected from that night. I knew secrets would be revealed, but I thought I was the only one revealing them, not her.

My heart went out to her when she told me about her past. I saw the pain in her eyes and I would have done anything to take it away for her. But I was powerless to change her past, just as I was powerless to change my present—to change what happened with Des.

Going into that night, I knew our relationship hung in the balance. I knew that my mistake with Des and my lies would jeopardize my relationship with Emma, and I had planned for any possible response Emma could have had when she heard the news. I thought I was prepared to tackle all of the possibilities to make sure we would remain together. What I didn't expect was her past and how it played into the consequences of my mistake with Des. What I didn't expect was to lose Emma, and to lose myself in the process.

During the weeks after that night in the rain, I did not give up on Emma. I thought that she just needed time to digest the information about Des's pregnancy, much like I did when I first found out. I thought that after a week or so, she would come around, we would work things out, and we would get back to normal.

But that didn't happen.

I tried calling her and texting her, but she wouldn't pick up. I stopped by her workstation once at work, and she told me not to bring in our personal issues into work or she would be forced to quit. After that day, I stopped bothering her at work. But I continued calling and texting. She continued to not respond to me.

Finally one night, I couldn't sleep. I felt an overwhelming need to see her and talk to her. Like a crazed man, I went to her place at three in the morning and rung the buzzer to her building. To my surprise, she picked up the buzzer.

"Hello?" Her voice sounded groggy. I must have awoken her.

"Emma, I need to see you," I begged.

"Brandon?" The groggy was immediately gone from her voice.

"Yes, can you let me in?"

"I don't think that's a good idea … I have nothing to say to you."

"Emma, please? I just don't understand why we can't be together. I'm not with Des. I'll always take care of the baby regardless of who I'm with." *Why couldn't she understand that?*

"Brandon, I don't expect you to understand this, but I hope you can respect my wishes on this. Please let me go. Please let us go," she said softly.

"But I can't let you do this. We love each other. I know this is not what you want."

There was silence for a moment.

"Brandon, I've moved on," she said coldly.

"What? What do you mean?"

"I'm with someone else now. His name's Damian. Please accept that we're over. Good night."

I heard her click off. I leaned my head against the intercom, my mind reeling from what she had just said.

*She's with someone else now? Damian? Wasn't he the guy she met at the bar when she called me in L.A.?*

My chest ached at the news. Could it be true? Could she really have moved on so quickly?

I went back home with a heavier heart. That night, I did not fall asleep.

# CHAPTER TWELVE

## *Emma*

It was three weeks since that night in the rain, the night my relationship with Brandon ended, the night my chances of the fairy tale ending with the man of my dreams shattered into a million pieces.

Brandon had tried to contact me a number of times since then, but I had managed to avoid most of his efforts. At work, I only saw him once a week at the weekly status conferences. But other than that, he had respected my wishes to be left alone, and had not approached me at work. While I was relieved, another part of me secretly wished that he would stop by and see me. That part of me desperately wanted to know how he was doing and what was going on in his life.

The last time he had tried contacting me was in the middle of the night last week. I was fast asleep when my buzzer went off. In my half-awake state, I answered the buzzer. It was Brandon. I knew I had to hurt him in order for him to let me go, in order for both of us to move on. I needed to move on, because each time he contacted me, a tiny piece of irrational hope fluttered into my heart, and each time, I was left devastated when I thought about the unborn child. So I lied to him. I told him that I had moved on. It had killed me to imagine how much that would have hurt him, but I knew that it was better than the prolonged pain of false hope we both shared.

I told the girls about our breakup, but only the part about Des being pregnant. I never told the girls—not even Jill—about my father. It had been a secret I have kept buried and locked in a deep vault inside me. I wouldn't have told Brandon if he hadn't pushed at a time where I was so vulnerable and wounded that I had to tell him. It was the one thing that I was ashamed of, the one thing I could never change about myself, and the one thing I hated about my life.

I occasionally hung out with Damian. Steph was right, he was a good distraction. He was wild and carefree, and when I was with him, I didn't have to think or feel. I never had sex with him though. I just couldn't. Damian seemed fine with that, but he was open with the fact that he was sleeping with other women. That was fine with me. I just needed someone to keep my mind off Brandon—to keep my heart frozen and numbed from pain.

But even with Damian keeping me busy, there were still moments where I would get a wave of longing for Brandon so strong, I found it difficult to draw breath.

My phone beeped. It was Damian: *Meet you at the steps of Union Square Park in 15?*

I responded: *Yup! See you there.*

It was the week before Christmas, and Damian and I were meeting up and helping each other with some last minute Christmas shopping around Union Square.

On my way out of my building, I checked the mail. There was a small package for me. It was from Jill's parents. *They're too sweet.* I excitedly opened the package and found an infinity dream necklace in a light blue, velvet pouch. Scrawled on a holiday card accompanying the necklace was a note from Gary and Sue, Jill's parents:

*Merry Christmas, Emma!*

*We hope this year has brought you much success and happiness in your life—in your career, in your health, and most importantly, in love. We saw this infinity dream necklace in a small shop in Verona, Italy—Italy's "City of Love." We immediately thought of you. You have always been a dreamer. So with this necklace, may all your dreams come true. We wish you a warm holiday season with lots of love and laughter.*

*Love always,*

*Gary & Sue*

Tears rolled down my face as I finished reading the note. Jill was just like her parents: kind, generous, and loving. I put on the round infinity dream necklace around my neck, and I smiled and felt a little more hopeful for the future.

I walked the six blocks down to Union Square from my place. It was a brisk December afternoon and the streets were bustling with shoppers. I sat on the steps of Union Square Park and smiled to myself as I took in the holiday decorations, festive music, and people all around me. The Christmas season always cheered me up.

"Hey gorgeous," came a husky voice from behind me. Damian pulled me in for a hug and kissed me on the cheek.

"Hey. Ready for some shopping?" I asked brightly.

He groaned. "No, but let's get it over with. Thanks for forcing me to do this."

"Of course. I need a distraction." I laughed.

Damian rolled his eyes. "I'm your go-to distraction."

"Well, most of my other distractions usually cost money. You're free," I teased.

"Right. Hm. I should start charging." He made a face at me and I laughed.

As we walked, I noticed all the girls we passed gaze lustfully at Damian. I turned and looked at him, and even though I saw the appeal, I did not feel the fast palpitations in my heart that I had felt with Brandon.

"Come on, let's go inside. It's getting a little chilly," I said as I pulled my trench coat tighter around me.

Damian put his arm around me and rubbed my arms.

"Thanks," I said, smiling at him warmly. "Why are you so nice to me?"

"Because you're like an innocent, lost puppy. I feel sorry for you," he teased.

"Hey! Don't be mean." I tried to playfully hit him, but before I knew it, my heels caught on a crack on the pavement, and I was falling forwards. Damian caught me just in time and helped me hop back two feet to where my shoe was trapped in the pavement. Damian pulled out the shoe and helped me put it on.

"Thanks," I beamed at him.

"No problem."

Just as I was straightening up, my breath caught when I saw him. Walking towards us half a block away was *Brandon*. He wasn't alone. Walking besides him was none other than Desiree. They both spotted me.

*God, I hope they didn't see me trip. Why am I such a klutz at the worst moments? I want to look elegant and hot in front of him—in front of her. Why did I have to trip now?* I sensed my face grow hot as they approached.

My eyes immediately spotted the bump on Des's stomach, and all my cheerfulness from minutes ago disappeared. I wanted to be anywhere else but here.

# CHAPTER THIRTEEN

## *Brandon*

I spotted her from a block away, before Des pointed her out. I saw her trip and wanted to be there to catch her. But I wasn't there. Instead, another guy was there to catch her. I saw him moments earlier with his arms around Emma, rubbing her arms with his hand. *Was this the Damian she mentioned the other night?* A jealous rage grew in the pit of my stomach. *That should be me with her.*

Then, as if she sensed me looking at her, she glanced over at me, and our eyes met. As we approached her and the guy, I could hear the rapid drumming of my heart beat against my chest. *God, I've missed her*, I thought as I looked at her. She took my breath away. I shifted my eyes and looked at the tall, built guy standing next to her, and a sharp pain twists in my chest. *She was no longer mine*, I thought. *She was no longer mine, and I had no one to blame but myself.*

When we were in front of them, we all gave each other fake, friendly smiles, as if we were greeting old friends.

"Hi. How are you?" I asked Emma.

"Good. You?" Her voice was overly cheerful as she looked between Des and then back to me. I saw the pain in her eyes that she tried so desperately to hide.

"Same." I resisted an overwhelming need to wrap my arms around her, to feel her, to kiss her, to smell her, to connect with her. I wanted a moment, however temporary, to hold her in my arms and imagine the perfect life we could have had together. My chest tightened at that thought—that wish that would never be fulfilled.

"Um. Well, this is Damian," she said, gesturing to the guy. I shook his hand and introduced myself, squeezing his hand harder than my normal handshakes. He responded by tightening his grip.

"Hey, man," Damian said to me. He looked at my coolly, like there was not a care in the world. *He is acting smug*, I thought. *He must know about me, and know that he got the woman that I want, but can't have.*

"I'm Des," came Des's cheerful voice besides me and she reached out and shook Emma's hand. I saw a gleam in her smile.

"Well," Emma said meekly as her eyes darted nervously around, focusing on everything—everything but me. There was a few seconds of silence as the awkward tension in the air made it hard to breathe. Emma then looked to her side at Damian. I noticed that his arm was around her again, which enraged me. "Well we should get going," she said as she turned away from me.

"Emma." I wanted her to look at me, to look into my eyes, to see—to know—how much I still loved her. She finally looked at me.

"Take care of yourself." I ended up saying. I wanted to tell her so much more, to go to her and hold her, to never let her go. Yet, something stopped me. Maybe the sadness that still lingered in her eyes when she looked at me, the sadness that I put there. It would have been selfish of me to keep pulling her into my life when I was going to have a child with Des. It was a mistake that I had to live with, but it wasn't one that Emma had to live with.

I loved her, more than I loved myself, and I knew I had to let her go. She would have a happier, uncomplicated life without me in it. She deserved to be happy—free from pain.

***

Anger, jealousy, and pain consumed me as I watched Emma walk away with that guy, his arms around her like she belonged to him. How did she move on so quickly? What did she see in him? The guy looked like bad news. He was not someone I wanted Emma to hang out with, let alone date. My chest tightened at the thought of them in bed together, of him inside her.

By the time I got to my car, I was fuming. Images of Emma happy with Damian flashed through my thoughts, images of him making her laugh, of him kissing her, of him making love to her, of her screaming his name. My hands gripped forcefully onto the steering wheel as I drove out of the parking garage. I felt sick to my stomach as jealousy took ahold of me.

Somewhere in the midst of my self-torment, I realized how quiet it was in the car. I looked over at Des, who was sitting in the passenger seat, staring blankly. She was looking out the window and I could only make out her profile. Her hands were gently rubbing the bump on her stomach. I realized something was wrong. She wasn't talking—not going on and on about plans for the baby and planning parenting classes for us. She sat there in complete silence.

"Des?"

She didn't respond.

"Des? What's wrong?" my voice more forceful.

Finally, she turned her face towards me, an ominous expression on her face. "Brandon we need to talk."

My stomach lurched at her words. What now?

# CHAPTER FOURTEEN

## Desiree

Panic coursed through me as we walked to the car. Did that bartender recognize me? I thought I saw a spark of recognition in his eyes.

*Shit!* He was going to tell her everything. She would know my secret.

I knew sooner or later this would happen, sooner or later I would get caught, sooner or later I would have to tell Brandon before he found out. And yet, at this moment, when my lies were bursting at the seams, threatening their way out into the open, I was still taken by surprise. I was still unprepared for this moment.

I looked over at Brandon, who was walking a few steps in front of me, immersed in thought.

*He was thinking about her again. He was always thinking about her.* I felt the all too familiar stench of jealousy flow through me.

*Who have I been fucking kidding? It would always be thoughts of her. It has been almost a month and things have not changed.* A sharp pang of sadness and loss washed through me.

Thoughts raced through my mind as I agonized over whether to tell Brandon, whether I was willing to lose everything I had worked so hard and so long for, everything that should have been rightfully mine.

For the last six months, guilt gripped my soul when I began down this path of lies. There were many moments of regret, moments where I wished I could have turn back time and changed what I had done, what I had said, and who I had hurt. I wished I could turn back time so I wouldn't hurt anymore—a hurt that was masked by this make-believe world I had created for myself, a world I created to shield myself from reality, a world where Brandon loved me and our unborn child.

*What was the point?* I sighed. The heaviness that had taken resident in my heart made it hard to feel any joy. I rubbed my stomach, and tears instantly filled my eyes.

I was exhausted. Mentally and emotionally. Exhausted in my efforts to try to win Brandon's love. It was a fool's errand. There was nothing for me to win.

Brandon may have been with me, spending time with me, taking care of me, but he wasn't the same Brandon I feel in love with when I was 16. He had changed into a man who was a stranger to me. A man who I had no feelings for.

I've changed too. My heart broke as the cold reality hit me: we weren't the same people we were when we loved each other. Those two people—that love—died with those memories long ago. My heart felt heavy as I mourned over my loss.

I saw the way he looked at Emma, and the way Emma looked at him. That was love—undeniable, heart-wrenching love. My heart ached at the realization that not only did Brandon no longer love me, but I no longer loved him. I had been holding onto something that wasn't love. I was just holding onto the past, a past where I felt safe, where I felt like I knew who I was and who loved me, where a whole future laid before me. But now, I had nothing, and I was desperate to fill that empty void.

"Des? What's wrong?" Brandon's voice broke through my thoughts.

I turned to him and realized that I had to come clean. "Brandon we need to talk."

I saw the panic in his eyes. *Is this how he sees me now? A bearer of bad news?*

"I need to tell you some things, but let's wait until we get back to your place. I want you to focus on your driving."

"Okay," he said hesitantly.

I knew he would never look at me the same after this conversation. It may very well be our last.

***

"So what is it that you want to talk about," Brandon asked me as he handed me a glass of water.

We were seated on the couch. I felt my heart race as I thought through how I was going to tell him everything.

I took a deep breath, trying to lessen the anxious energy that coursed through me. My hands nervously played with the fringes of the throw that laid next to me on the couch. Brandon eyed me nervously, patiently waiting for me to say something.

"So, do you remember when you called me last April on my birthday? It was after you came back from your business trip in Cancun."

"Yeah, of course," he said with a nod. "What about it?"

"You had mentioned that you met a girl there. You said she was sweet and silly, and you thought there was something there."

"I told you that?"

"Yes, you did," I paused before continuing. "Well, I knew just by the way you talked about her that she was something special, different from the other girls you've mentioned before." I felt the familiar ache in my chest at the memory.

"Oh," he said slowly. I could see his thoughts racing to her, remembering his time with her in Cancun.

"I was jealous, and … I was afraid to lose you …" my voice trailed off.

"Des, what are you trying to tell me?" He looked at me nervously.

"When my dad passed away this summer, I felt like I had lost everything. I felt like I had lost everyone who loved me. I just couldn't bear the idea that I was losing you too." I quickly brushed away a tear that rolled down my cheek.

"Okay," he said anxiously.

"When I called you that night after his funeral, I was in a bad place. I felt self-destructive and got really drunk."

"Yeah, I remember. You were a mess," he said sympathetically.

I sighed. "Yeah, I was. Well, I bought a pill off someone to numb the pain, a pill to help me black out. ..." I looked up at him and saw the worry in his eyes.

"Des, you can't do that to yourself," he said.

"I know. I was very grateful that I had the sense to call you before I took the pill and hurt myself. You rescued me that night. You were gentle and loving, and ... and in my drunken state, I wanted you back. I wanted you to love me the way you had before—the way no one else has since. I ... I slipped you the pill instead." I looked away from him in shame.

"What?" Shock covered Brandon's face as he processed what I just said. "Des! What are you saying? What kind of pill did you give me? How come I don't remember this?" he asked me incredulously.

"I roofied you," I admitted softly.

"You what?" his voice was sharp, causing me to flinch.

"I'm so sorry. I wasn't in a good place and I was drunk."

"Des, that's not an excuse!"

"I know. I know. But while you were taking care of me, I convinced myself that it was a good idea to roofie you and to get you to sleep with me. I … I thought that once we made love, you would realize how much you actually still loved me. I thought we would be able to rekindle our relationship, and be happy again. … I wanted desperately to be happy again." My voice was shaky and tears streamed down my face.

"Fuck. I don't believe it," he said in a whisper. "You're pregnant because you roofied me?" his voice increasing in volume. "How could you, Des?" There was no anger in his voice, only disappointment and disbelief. This tore at my heart. I knew I had lost him forever—not just his love, but his friendship.

"There's more," I whispered.

"What more can there be?" His eyes became more alert as he waited for me to continue.

"We … we didn't have sex that night."

"What?" His voice was loud and harsh, and I flinched. "But—"

"When I roofied you, you blacked out pretty quickly. I undressed you and got you to your bed. But … but when I tried to get you hard, it didn't work." I felt ashamed of myself.

I saw Brandon's mouth open and close a few times as he tried to say something. Finally, he asked, "Why didn't you say something? Why did you let me believe we had sex?"

I looked away in shame. "I don't know. I think part of me hoped that, even if we didn't have sex, if you thought we did, you would rethink your feelings for me, and maybe you would realize that you still loved me."

He remained silent and I could tell he was struggling between a number of emotions. "So … I'm not the father of the baby," he said as he looked at the bump on my stomach.

My heart was beating violently against my chest. *Could he handle yet another confession?* I drew in a deep breath and said, "I'm … I'm not pregnant." I reached behind my back and pulled against the hook that held the belly-support belt and padding against my stomach. Brandon's eyes went wide with shock as he saw me remove the padding and belt from under my shirt.

"Holy shit," he muttered as he brushed his hand through his hair in shock.

"I'm so sorry, Brandon. I—"

"Why?" he yelled, cutting me off. "Why, Des?"

Shame washed through me. "I didn't want to lose you," I whispered.

"That doesn't make sense." He looked at me in disbelief.

"When I dropped by your place a few months ago, I was in town and wanted to surprise you. I was also hoping that we could spend some time together. But when I saw Emma at the door wearing nothing but your shirt and boxers, I was in shock. I don't know what came over me, but I blurted out that you were my boyfriend. And once she ran off, I realized there was no turning back. I didn't want to tell you what I said to her. I didn't want you to look at me like you're looking at me now."

There was a moment of silence before Brandon finally spoke. "How long were you planning on holding onto this lie, Des? What were you going to do when nine months passed and you had no baby to show for?"

"I don't know. I hadn't thought that far ahead at the time. I … I thought that maybe you would fall back in love with me, and then I could say that I lost the child," I murmured.

"That's just nuts, Des." Brandon shook his head as he tried to take everything in.

"I'm so sorry, Brandon. I don't expect you to forgive me. I'm … I'm just sorry. I didn't want to hurt anyone, but I know I did."

He remained silent at my words, whether it was in shock or in deep thought, I couldn't tell.

"Please say something!" I begged. "Please yell at me! Please talk to me!"

"I can't really look at you right now, Des. I trusted you! I believed everything you had told me. We have known you for over 11 years, and we've been through so much together. I didn't think I needed to question anything you said because it was *you*—the one person who has been there for me at my darkest days."

"I know. I didn't want to lie to you. I shouldn't have …"

"I—I don't know what to think or say right now. I don't know who you are anymore!"

"I'm still the same person," I cried. "I just made a huge mistake."

"I don't know, Des. I'm so angry at you. Do you know how much drama you've caused?" I heard the pain in his voice, and my heart ached. He was the last person I wanted to disappoint and upset. The last person I wanted to hurt.

"I'm really sorry," I whispered.

Suddenly, something changed in his expression. "I can't do this right now," he said with a flash of urgency. "I need to go."

"Go?"

"Yes. I need to find Emma. I need to tell her everything. I need to tell her everything before she falls for…" His voice trailed off. I felt a stab in my heart when I heard him say her name. *His thoughts always go to her.*

Without another word, Brandon ran out the door, leaving me sitting in his condo. I knew that I had lost him forever. I knew that I was again alone.

## CHAPTER FIFTEEN

*Emma*

"What do you mean you've met Des before?" Shock roared through me as we got to my apartment. I had broken my heel when my shoe got stuck in the pavement, so we had walked to my place a few blocks away so I could switch shoes.

"Yeah, I've seen her at the bar once," Damian said.

"How come you didn't tell me?" I looked at him with disbelief.

"Shit, Emma. Chill. I didn't know her name. And even if I did, how the hell would I know it's the same Desiree you've been telling me about?"

"Oh. Right. Sorry," I looked at him sheepishly. "Sorry, that woman just seems to have a way of getting under my skin."

He laughed. "Yeah, I can see that."

"Sorry, I didn't mean to lash out at you."

"It's cool. No sweat," he said coolly.

"What was she doing at the bar?" I asked. Despite the fact that it pained me to think about Desiree, the masochist in me wanted to know every excruciating detail about this woman.

Damian laughed. "What do people usually do at a bar? Drink, of course."

"Are you sure it was her?" I asked skeptically.

"Yeah, it was her."

"But how can you be sure?"

"I don't forget a pretty face, and she's hot."

"Hey!" I hit Damian on the arm.

"What?" he asked innocently.

"You're suppose to be on my side," I said defensively.

"Who said anything about sides? I'm a man-whore remember? She's hot. I'd bang her," he said matter-of-factly.

I made a face.

He laughed. "I offered to bang you too, but you rejected me." He feigned a frown.

I rolled my eyes, and then asked, "When did you see her at the bar?" I didn't understand why Des would be drinking when she was pregnant. And if Damian saw her at the bar before she was pregnant, why was she in SF during that time? From what Brandon had told me, she only recently moved here from L.A.

"Hmm, I think like a month or so ago, about two weeks before you and your friends were at my bar."

"But …" My mind raced as I pieced together the timeline, "that's when she told Brandon she was pregnant …"

"Yeah, now that you mention it, that sounds familiar. She came into the bar in the late morning that day when we had just opened. I remembered thinking that it wasn't the typical time of the day for a girl like her to want to get plastered. She was talking about how her ex was with someone else now. She was upset that he had refused to get back together with her, even after she had told him she was pregnant with his child."

I tried to absorb this new information Damian just told me. "She wanted him back," I whispered to myself. Then I looked at Damian, "She was getting drunk? Are you sure?"

"Yes, I'm sure. It's not every day you have a pregnant woman getting drunk at the bar. After she mentioned that she was pregnant, I refused to serve her. She then said she really wasn't pregnant."

I looked at him in disbelief. "She's not pregnant?" I was shell-shocked by this news. "Are you sure she wasn't lying about that just to get drunk?"

"Yeah, I'm sure. I had asked her how she was going to pull off being pregnant, and she mentioned something about a padded baby bump or something that you can buy."

"It's fake," I whispered as my thoughts raced at the news and what this all meant.

"Ohmygod, do you know what this means?"

"Um, that she's not pregnant?" he asked uncertainly.

"Yes! It means she's not pregnant!" I yelled excitedly.

He laughed. "But I've just told you that."

"I know. It didn't sink in when you said it. She's not pregnant!" I squealed. "Damian, thank you thank you! I got to go!" I cried out as I put on a pair of flats and ran out of my apartment.

"What? I thought we're going shopping?" Damian yelled after me.

"Sorry! Rain check! Call you later!"

I needed to see Brandon now. I needed to tell him this in person. If this was all true, then we can be together again. I felt an overwhelming rush of joy at that thought. Maybe I haven't lost Brandon forever after all.

***

Ten minutes later, I was taking the elevator up to Brandon's condo on the penthouse floor of his building. Anxiety and delirious giddiness built inside me during the cab ride over. I wasn't sure what I was going to say to Brandon, but I knew I wanted to see him. I knew I wanted to tell him how much I've missed him, how much I still loved him.

When the elevator doors opened, I rushed to his door and pressed the buzzer.

No answer.

I pressed it again.

Nothing.

I pulled out my phone and decided to call him. I felt an irresistible pull towards him, a desperate need to connect with him in some form. Just as I was about to pull up his number, my phone started peeping. It was *Brandon*!

"Hello? Brandon?" I said breathlessly into my phone.

"Emma. Where you are?" His voice was rush, full of life and urgency.

"Um. I was actually going to ask you the same thing," I laughed.

"Oh, really?"

"Yeah! I'm ... I'm at your place," I admitted.

"You are? Why?"

"I needed to talk to you. Where are you?" I asked.

He laughed. "This is going to sound crazy, but I'm at *your* place. I called you because you didn't answer your intercom buzzer."

"Oh, really?" I felt a surge of happiness overwhelm me.

"Yeah. Stay where you are! I'll be right over, okay?" he said in a rush.

"Okay!" I exclaimed.

I hung up the phone and squealed with excitement. *Did he know something too? Why else was he over at my place?*

"I was going to see him," I said out loud. As I impatiently waited for him to arrive, I thought about what I wanted to say, how I wanted to tell him.

As I paced up and down the empty hallway, I began to feel hot. As I took off my trench coat, somewhere in the back of my mind, I remembered something Brandon had once said to me: "*You're the only person I would want showing up unannounced at my place, and preferably in a trench coat and nothing else.*"

I looked at the trench coat in my hands, and giggled. I quickly stripped off all my clothes and put my trench coat back on. I managed to fit all my clothes inside my tote bag when I heard the elevator door ping.

A surge of excitement flooded through me. *He's here!*

He came out of the elevator, and he was alone. When I saw the same deliriously-happy look in his eyes, I knew that he somehow also found out. I dropped my tote bag and ran towards him.

"You know?" he asked with his arms outstretched to greet me.

"Yes, I know!" I exclaimed as I jumped into his embrace, my legs hugging his waist as he pulled my face down with his hands and kissed me passionately, our mouths greeting each other like old lovers.

"God, you have no ideas how much I've missed you," he sighed.

"I've missed you, too," I cried. "It's been almost unbearable without you."

"What about Damian?" he asked. I heard the jealousy in his voice.

"He's just a friend. I lied about being with him so that you could move on. I'm sorry," I whispered. I leaned down and kissed him tenderly, my arms around his neck as his hands moved up and down my back.

"How did you find out?" I asked.

"Des told me."

I looked at him in surprise. "Really?" I asked doubtfully. "What did she tell you?"

"That she's not pregnant, and we didn't have sex that night."

"What? You guys didn't have sex?"

"No, we didn't. I had blacked out and didn't remember anything from that night. So when I woke up with her in my bed, I thought we did have sex. She said we did. But today, she told me the truth. We never had sex that night."

I heard the relief in his voice, and I felt the same relief melt away any remaining worries I had about whether there was still something between them.

"How did you find out?" he asked.

"Coincidentally, through Damian. He's a bartender at a bar, and he remembered seeing Des there recently. She was drinking and said something about faking a pregnancy."

"Wow," he said. For a moment, I saw a sadness in his eyes.

"Is she okay?" I asked, wondering what kind of state she must be in to tell Brandon the truth.

"I'm not sure, but I think so."

Brandon smiled at me and asked, "So, does this mean we can finally be together again?" His tone was teasing.

"Do you really need to ask that question?" I giggled.

He smiled at me widely. *God, I forgot how much those dimples affected me.* He looked at me affectionately without saying a word.

"What?" I asked.

"Nothing. It's just so nice to hear you laugh," he said. "I've really missed that."

"I've really missed this," I whispered as I pulled him down towards me for another kiss, parting my lips and taking his tongue into my mouth. As our lips moved rhythmically together, he lifted me up from the ground and moved me towards his door.

As we moved, the front of my trench coat shifted to the side, revealing my left breast. Brandon inhaled sharply and looked at me, his eyes were ablaze with lust. "You're naked." His voice was ragged, and I knew I wanted him now.

I gave him a seductive smile as I pulled his body closer against me, "Weren't you the one who said that if I ever show up unannounced, you'd prefer me to be in a trench coat and nothing else?"

"There's nothing under there?" he asked. "God, you're driving me crazy," he growled as he fumbled for his keys from his pocket.

I shook my head as the insatiable need for him overtook me. "No, I need you now."

"Let's me get this door." I can hear the hunger in his voice.

"Fuck the door," I gasped. "We're on the penthouse floor. You're the only unit on this floor."

Before he could respond, I removed my trench coat, dropping it to the floor, and started grinding my naked body against him. He immediately gave in, and in a blink of an eye, he had me pinned against the wall, anchoring my hands together above my head with one hand. I gasped as his mouth circled the center of my breast, licking and flicking his tongue around my nipples. I curled my right leg around him and pulled him against me, feeling his erection dig into me through his jeans.

"God, Emma. You're pushing me to the edge," he groaned.

"Good," I whispered. "Let me undress you," I purred.

He released his stronghold on my hands. I pulled his body around, moving his back against the wall. I gave him a wicked smile and whispered, "My turn."

As I unbuttoned his jeans, I leaned into him and kissed him violently, biting his lower lip and smoothing each bite with my tongue. I unzipped his jeans and my hands moved inside his boxers. I inhaled sharply when I found him. He was rock hard and ready. I looked at him and saw my frenzy reflected in the gleam in his eyes.

"I want to taste you," I whispered as I pulled his jeans down, his erection sprung out from inside his boxers to greet me.

I traced the outline of his manhood lightly with my fingertips, looking up at him to see his reactions. Without warning, I wrapped my hands around him and moved up and down his length, causing him to throw back his head in pleasure. As his eyes were closed, I took him into my mouth, catching him by surprise. His body spasm and he groaned in the throes of pleasure. He was soft, hard, and long. I looked up at him as my mouth slowly and laboriously explored the entire length of him. His eyes glowed and smoldered with pleasure. I knew he wanted me to go faster, but I didn't. I wanted to tease him a little longer. I wanted him to want me more. I wanted him to come harder.

"My God, you feel so fucking incredible." His voice was strained as he jerked each time I reached the base of his erection. "I can't hold on much longer," he groaned.

I looked up at him and gave him a sinful smile, "How would you like to come?"

"That's easy," he said with a ragged voice as he pulled me up from the ground and pressed my body hard against his. "Inside you."

We lowered ourselves on the lush carpeted floor and he climbed on top of me. I stopped him.

"No," I resisted. "I want to be on top," I purred. I wanted to be in control this time.

His eyes were filled with molten intensity as he laid on his back and looked up at me. I felt all the blood rushing down between my legs as I straddled him. A need built inside of me as I felt his manhood against my wet, sensitive skin. His hands reached out and massaged with my breast, causing moans to escape my lips.

"God, I could never get tired of this view," he said as he admired my naked body on top of him. "Move for me, baby."

I moved my hips against his erection in slow, long sweeping movements, never allowing him to enter me.

"You're such a tease," he groaned as he moved his pelvis against me. A moan escaped my lips as I felt his erection hard against my inner thigh. My body throbbed in anticipation of him inside me.

Finally, I guided his entire length deep inside me in one slow and hungry thrust. My back arched in pleasure as I felt my body expand for him.

"Fuck, Emma. You feel *incredible*. I can't take this anymore," he growled. I gasped when his hands griped tightly around my hips and he pounded upwards inside me. First slow, but with each thrust, he drove into me deeper and harder. My hips rocked against him as he moved me in time with his up-thrusts.

Then, before I registered what happened, he flipped me around and I was on my back. "Let me take the reins, baby," he growled. I arched my hips up against him, begging for him to move deeper inside me. He gave me a lust-filled smile as he pounded himself inside me, causing me to gasp with pleasure.

It didn't take long before I felt my inner muscles tightened around his hardness. "I'm about to come," I gasped. I looked up at him and saw the raw hunger in his eyes. He pounded into me harder until I began to spasm. I dug my nails into his muscular back as he entered me one last time before he began to convulse inside me. As if in response to him, my body began to shake uncontrollably as I reached the peak of ecstasy, and as I screamed his name in pleasure, my whole body was consumed with ecstasy as we crash together into the abyss.

In the afterglow, I sighed with contentment. I finally had Brandon in my arms and inside me, where he belonged.

As my breathing slowed our rendezvous with ecstasy, I looked deviously at Brandon. "Let's do it again," I purred. "Maybe somewhere a little more comfortable ... and private this time."

"Baby, you read my mind," he groaned. He got up and picked me up from the floor and carried me into his condo.

And for the rest of the day, we stayed in his bed, and we made love.

Not once, not twice, but three earthshattering times.

# CHAPTER SIXTEEN

## Six Months Later

### *Brandon*

"Are you sure you want to do this?" asked Emma warily.

I quickly glanced from the road to her as I took her hand and squeezed it reassuringly. "Stop worrying, babe. Of course I want to meet your mom. We've been dating for over six months now. You can't hide me from her forever?" I joked.

"I'm know. Sorry, I'm just nervous. I've never brought a guy home to see her before, and ..." Her voice trailed off.

"Emma, it'll be fine," I reassured her. "I'm sure she'll love me," I teased.

She giggled nervously, "That's pretty cocky of you, Mr. Fisher."

"Well, you know me," I played along, giving her a wink and a wide smile. "Women love me."

She smacked my shoulder, "Hey!"

I chuckled, "Sorry, sorry. Low blow. You know I didn't mean that," I said apologetically. "I ... I know you're nervous about this, and I just wanted to lighten things up. I—"

"I know," she interrupted. "I just want things to go well today."

"And it will," I reassured her. I knew why Emma was nervous, and I was nervous too. From what I knew about Emma's mom's past, I had a feeling she didn't put a great deal of trust with men. I needed her mom to like me and approve of my relationship with Emma. It was important to Emma, and it was important to me.

I wanted this weekend to go perfectly. It was Friday night after work and we were going to Emma's mom's house in Sacramento for dinner. Tomorrow, we were heading up to Napa Valley for the rest of the weekend. We were staying at a villa my family owned, and I have been planning this special weekend for a while now. Because this weekend, I was going to ask Emma to marry me.

***

"The meal was absolutely delicious, Ms. Anderson," I smiled warmly at Emma's mom, whose eyes twinkled the way Emma's did. "Now I know where Emma gets her amazing cooking talents." I smiled over at Emma, who still looked a little nervous.

"Thanks, Brandon. And please, I insist that you call me June," she smiled at me. "I'm so glad you were able to come and visit."

I looked at June and could tell where Emma got her features from.

"Me too. Emma tells me how hard you've work to raise her, and it's so great that Emma has an amazing mother like you."

June smiled at me. "That's very kind of you, Brandon. Emma told me you lost your mother at a young age. That must have been hard."

I nodded.

"Well, I can tell just from our short time together that she did a wonderful job when she was still around in raising you."

"Thank you, that means a lot," I said, touched by her words.

"Mom, Brandon and I were talking and we'd love for you to come to SF sometime for a visit." Emma beamed at me.

"It's close enough for a day trip, but you can also stay for a weekend or a week. There's plenty of things to do," I chimed in.

"And I'd love for you to see Brandon's condo," Emma said.

"*Our* condo," I corrected, smiling at Emma. Emma moved in with me a month ago, and it's been amazing having her around. I hadn't realized what was missing from my home until she showed up. Now, my condo felt warm and inviting and homey—the way Emma makes me feel.

Emma blushed at my comment.

I turned to June. "You see, the agreement is, I take care of the mortgage and bills, and she takes care of everything food related. I'm not to be trusted in the kitchen. And between you and me, I think she has the much harder job." I looked over at Emma and smiled.

June laughed. "Well, that sounds lovely. I'll look at my calendar and see if I can take off some time." she smiled as she looked between Emma and me.

"Will you excuse me?" Emma got up from her chair, "I'm going to the restroom." We watched Emma walk down the hall.

I knew this was the time to ask her.

I turned to June. "June, I want to thank you for your hospitality."

"Of course Brandon, you're such a gentleman. Emma says so many great things about you."

I smiled. "She says amazing things about you as well. Before she gets back, I wanted to ask you something."

"Sure, what is it?"

"I want to let you know that I love your daughter. Very much. She is my world. She makes me laugh and feel. She is an amazing person. I have a romance weekend planned for her this weekend. I want to know if I have your blessing to ask your daughter to marry me."

"Oh! That's wonderful news. Of course! Brandon, I can tell you're a genuine guy, and you adore Emma. I see the looks you two give each other, and I know you guys love each other very much. You of course have my blessing." I saw the happiness in June's eyes, and for a second, I saw a piece of Emma in her.

"Thank you. Thank you so much."

A sense of relief washed over me at June's words. I worried about this moment more than I had admitted to Emma. I wanted June's approval because, like my own mother to me, June's approval meant the world to Emma. I could not imagine asking Emma to marry me before getting her mother's blessing.

***

Nerves shot through me as I thought over in my mind what I wanted to say to her. For the third time in the last ten minutes, I found myself unconsciously reaching over to the breast pocket of my blazer to make sure that small box was still there.

Then, I heard her approach from afar and a rush of excitement and anxiety flooded through me. I wanted everything to be perfect for her. I loved this woman with all my heart and soul, and today would be one of the memories we would cherish for the rest of our lives together.

I grabbed the guitar and began to strum a melody as I saw her walking towards me.

## CHAPTER SEVENTEEN
### *Emma*

"Where is he?" I thought as I walked back to the living room in the villa. There was a warm fire crackling in the fireplace in the far corner and the heat from the fire caressed my cool cheeks. Brandon had asked me to grab the two bottles of wine that we had accidentally left in the car from today's wine tasting. When I left a few minutes ago, he was sitting in the living room. But now, he was gone.

"Brandon?" I called out.

Nothing.

"Brandon? Where are you?"

Again nothing.

Then, something on the coffee table in front of the fireplace caught my eye. It was a small white cue card that said, "Follow the lights."

I looked around, trying to figure out what the note is talking about. And then I saw it, about 10 feet away, on a side table was another small white cue card. I walked over and saw an arrow drawn on the card, pointing towards patio.

When I got to the patio, I saw a trail of small lanterns on the floor leading out into the vineyard, each lantern two feet from the last.

I followed the trail and found myself behind the house walking next to the grape vineyard. I pulled my shawl wrap around my body as the brisk wind blew through the rows of grapevines. It was dusk and besides the departing crimson sun peeking through the horizon, the sky was entirely dark. A gentle, grey half-moon was making its ascent into the night sky.

As I walked, I heard a soft melody playing. I looked around, searching for the source. Then I found it. On the edge of the vineyard, there was a group of three leafless trees surrounding a picnic table. Two dozen lanterns hung from the various branches of the trees, lighting up the area with soft light. Next to the picnic table was a few logs burning in a small fire.

Standing next to the table was Brandon, playing "A Thousand Years" by Christina Perri on a guitar. He was looking at me, and I saw the love and emotion in eyes as he took my breath away.

I walked to him as he serenaded me. By the time I got to his side, I was in tears. "What is all this?" I asked softly.

He put the guitar down and held out his hands. Our fingers weaved into one and I felt the electric connection pulse between us. "Well, you mentioned once that you loved a guy who can serenade you with a guitar." He smiled at me, and I melted into his gaze. Even after this much time, I was still affected by his presence.

"But I thought you didn't know how to play?"

"I didn't. But I took some lessons," he said as he beamed at me.

"Why?" I asked. But I knew I didn't need him to say it out loud. I already knew, and tears filled my eyes.

Then, Brandon knelt down on one knee, and tears began to blind me as I knew what was coming. "Because I love you, Emma. Because I want to be the man you will love more and more each day. Because every day I'm with you, I fall in love with you more and more. I could never have imagined having this much love for anyone. I couldn't until I met you."

I saw him draw a nervous breath, and I beamed down at him.

"Emma," he said as he held my hands, "I loved you the second you walked into my life. Not too many people can experience this kind of love. Would you make my dreams come true, and marry me?"

He opened a small boxed, and I gasped. Inside the box was a vintage emerald cut diamond ring.

"Yes! Yes! A million times yes!" I exclaimed, my eyes full of tears. I pulled Brandon up and our lips met in a tender and passionate kiss.

"Brandon, I loved you the second you walked into my dreams. I cannot imagine marrying anyone else," I whispered.

We looked into each other's eyes and I knew that we were meant to spend forever together. There was an unspoken understanding in his eyes, and I knew that he loved me—that he had always loved me, and will always love me.

# EPILOGUE

## *Brandon*

I inhaled deeply, trying to steady the nervous energy that ran through me. The air smelled sweet of an intoxicating mixture of deep pink peonies, white gardenias, and blush pink tea roses—Emma's favorites. A crisp, spring breeze blew through the air, bellowing through the delicate layers of fabric and ribbons that danced around me, bringing soothing rhythmic sounds to my ears. I glanced up and saw the golden sun beginning its decent over the clear blue sky. Today was perfect.

Today was *finally* here. The day that I've been waiting a long time for. The day that I would finally marry my soul mate. The day that I could finally call Emma my wife. I smiled broadly, unable to contain the all-consuming happiness that radiated through me.

I looked out at the crowd of family and friends seated in rows of gold Chiavari chairs, all waiting with me for the love of my life to walk down the rose petal-covered aisle.

Emma's mom caught my eye. She beamed at me with tears in her eyes. She held her hands to her chest and gave me a warm, reassuring smile. Her approval meant the world to me, just as much as my own mother's approval would have meant to me if she were here. I was then filled with a warm sense of calm, as if I was being hugged from the inside. I smiled as tears welled up in my eyes. She *was* here, and she knew how happy I was.

The string quartet began to softly play Pachelbel's *Canon in D* and everyone turned their attention to the other end of the aisle. I exhaled deeply to calm my nerves, anxiously brushing my palms along my side, and watched as the wedding procession started.

Then, walking out of the French doors and into the courtyard came Emma in the arms of my father. The vision of her, in the winter white Vera Wang strapless gown that cascaded to the floor in waves of organza, took my breath away. She was radiant.

She met my gaze and beamed at me, her cheeks flushed and her eyes twinkled with excitement. She was absolutely beautiful, and at that moment, she was all that existed in my world. Everything else blurred into the background, and she was the only person I saw. It was just Emma and me. Us and our future.

I watched with bated breath as she walk slowly towards me. I could tell that she was nervous as she held onto my father's arm. I quickly glanced at my father, the amazing man who had always been there for me, even when I hadn't always wanted him to. And now, he was the amazing man who would always be there for Emma—the father that she never had. I felt another wave of emotions as I remembered the moment when Emma asked my father to walk her down the aisle.

When she finally got to my side, she whispered, "How did I do?"

I chuckled lightly, knowing that I was probably the only that would know what she meant. "As elegant as ever," I whispered as I gave her a wink. She smiled sweetly at me and we held hands and looked towards the officiant.

"Good afternoon, everyone," said Gary, Jill's father, who we had asked to be the one to marry us. "We are gathered here to celebrate a special union of love between Brandon Jonathan Fisher and Emma Sue Anderson." As Gary introduced us, my eyes never left Emma's and hers never left mine. She squeezed my hands and I felt the intensity of pure love flow through us.

"Do you, Brandon, take Emma to be your lawful wedded wife?"

"I do," I said.

"And do you, Emma, take Brandon to be your lawful wedded husband?"

"I do," she said as she beamed at me with tears in her eyes.

"Brandon and Emma have each prepared their own vows that they would like to say before they exchange rings." Gary gestured towards me.

I held Emma's left hand in one hand and the ring in the other and smiled at her. "Emma. For the longest time, I felt empty and incomplete, like something was missing in my life. But when I met you and then got to know you, I realized that you were the missing piece to my puzzle. You are what makes me whole, and I can't imagine a life without you. There are many endearing qualities about you that I *love*. You are one of the sweetest people I've ever meet. You care, and I mean, *really* care about those around you, and you feel with all of your heart and soul. You are also one of the most accident-prone people I've ever met. I will always remember and cherish our first coffee moment," I chuckled and winked at her. She flushed and smiled at me.

"Please accept this ring as a token of my love and commitment to you. May its presence on your finger remind you of my eternal love for you. There may be times when I fail you, when I upset you, and when I hurt you. But when those times come, please remember that I will love you until my last dying breath, and please forgive me for those failures. I cannot image my life without you in it."

I slid the ring into Emma's finger with tears in my eyes.

Emma gently brushed the tears from her own eyes and looked up at me. "Brandon, I've always heard of that all-consuming type of love that can change you as a person. I thought that this type of love was just a fairy tale. I never thought that I, of all people, would find that love myself—not until I met you. You are strong when I am weak, patient when I am hasty, determined when I have given up. You never lost sight of what we could be, and no matter how much I pushed you away, you were always there to catch me. And for that, I am eternally grateful."

Tears streamed down her face, and my chest tightened as I thought about the days when I thought I had lost her. *I love you*, I mouthed to her.

"Please accept this ring as a token of my love and pledge to you. May its presence on your finger remind you of my eternal love for you. I know there will be times in the future where tears will be shed from our eyes. Whether they are tears of sorrow or, like today, tears of joy, please know that I will always be by your side to embrace those tears with you."

"Brandon and Emma." Gary smiled at us warmly. "May you live happily ever after. May all your days be blessed with love, friendship, and laughter. And may all of your dreams come true as you journey through life together, because in dreams and in love, there are no impossibilities. By the power vested in me by the state of California, I now pronounce you husband and wife. You may now kiss the bride."

Before Gary's last sentence was spoken, I pulled Emma towards me and our lips locked in an all-consuming, passionate kiss. And for just a moment, I felt like time stopped and the world stood still to celebrate the magic of our union.

\*\*\*

## Emma

Today was perfect—more perfect than I could have ever imagined it to be. I was now officially Mrs. Brandon Fisher. I squealed inside at this thought. I never thought this moment would happen—the moment where all my dreams came true.

"Are you ready, Mrs. Fisher?" whispered Brandon as he leaned down and kissed my forehead.

I beamed at him. "As ready as I'll ever be, Mr. Fisher. You know dancing and being a klutz don't really go hand and hand. Just make sure I don't trip over my dress," I joked nervously.

"I'll try. But honestly, with your track record, I'm not sure that's humanly possible," he teased.

"Hey, be nice to your wife!" I hit his chest playfully, and he used this opportunity to pull me towards him. "Don't worry. If you trip, your husband will be there to catch you. He'll *always* be there to catch you." He leaned down and kissed me, and I felt all my worries and nerves melt away.

"Ladies and gentlemen, please welcome Brandon and Emma onto the dance floor for their first dance together as husband and wife."

"Ready?" asked Brandon.

I nodded and smiled nervously.

Brandon led me onto the dance floor, which sat in the middle of the transparent canopy tents that covered the entire reception area.

As soft music started playing and Nat King Cole began to sing "L-O-V-E" over the speakers, we started swirling effortlessly around the dance floor, getting lost into the music.

The reception area felt magical. Antiqued votive holders were scattered throughout the canopy tent, string lights covered every inch of the tent's ceiling, and pendant lights hung from the rafters. As we moved around the dance floor, it felt like we were dancing among the stars.

I looked into Brandon's eyes, and my heart was filled with a delirious joy that brought tears to my eyes. He leaned down and kissed a tear on my cheek, and I sighed contently. He held me tighter around him and I felt my body mold perfectly with his.

"I love you, Brandon Fisher, the man of my dreams."

We laughed at our inside joke.

"I love you, Emma Fisher. I will *always* love you. Forever and always."

He smiled, leaned closer to me, and whispered, "And this is *not* a dream."

I smiled back at him, and knew he was right. This could not be a dream. This was better than any dream could ever be.

## The End

*Due to popular demand from readers, Damian, the self-proclaimed man-whore, has his own two-book series!* **Damian** *is book one is* **The Heartbreaker** *series and is now available.*

## PLAYLIST FOR EMMA'S SERIES

My writing process would not be the same without music. The following are only some of the songs that have helped shape *A Night to Forget* and *The Day to Remember*. These songs are in order of how I have imagined them in this series, so if you wanted to have some fun, you could try and match up these songs with the scenes you believe they go with.

The music videos playlist can be found here http://goo.gl/rWkSQC. I encourage you to check out these artists and support them and their talent.

### *A Night to Forget*

"Dream" – Priscilla Ahn

"Anything Could Happen" – Ellie Goulding

"Mountain Sound" – Of Monsters and Men

"I Knew I Loved You" – Savage Garden

"I Can't Make You Love Me" – Bonnie Raitt

"Cold Shoulder" – Adele

"I Can't Help Falling in Love With You" – Elvis Presley

"If You're Not The One" – Daniel Bedingfield

"Bubbly" – Colbie Caillat

"A Thousand Years" – Christina Perri **[Theme Song]**

"Call Your Girlfriend" – Robyn

## *The Day to Remember*

"I Can't Help Falling In Love With You" (instrumental) – Instrumental Music Brothers

"Punching In a Dream" – The Naked and Famous

"Almost Lover" – A Fine Frenzy

"I Won't Back Down" – Tom Petty and The Heartbreakers

"You Were Mine" – Dixie Chicks

"Never Say Never" – The Fray

"Last Request" – Paolo Nutini

"It Will Rain" – Bruno Mars

"Someone Like You" – Adele

"Mr. Brightside" – The Killers

"How Do I Live Without You" – LeAnn Rimes

"Better Together" – Jack Johnson

"A Thousand Years" – Boyce Avenue acoustic cover **[Brandon's serenade]**

"Marry Me" – Train

"L-O-V-E" – Nat King Cole

## OTHER BOOKS

If you would like to stay informed of new releases, giveaways, and news on upcoming books, please sign up for Jessica Wood's mailing list:

http://jessicawoodauthor.com/mailing-list/.

If you enjoyed reading *The Day to Remember*, I would love it if you could help others enjoy this novel as well by recommending and/or reviewing this novel.

In addition to *The Day to Remember*, book two in the *Emma's Story* series, here is a list of my other books:

*Emma's Story*: Book #1: *A Night to Forget*

*Summer Fling* – an anthology of short stories from six authors.

*Damian*

***

**Below is a synopsis for Damian:**

**Meet Damian Castillo. The man, the legend, the heartbreaker.**

As a self-proclaimed man-whore, Damian doesn't believe in love or commitment. In fact, he can't remember the last time he's had feeling for a woman that went beyond hot, no-strings-attached sex. The only things he cares about are his bar, his appearance, and his needs.

But then he meets Alexis.

Meet Alexis Blythe. A small town girl that has lost a lot of love in her life. Wanting to leave her past behind her, she moves to San Francisco looking for a big change. Yet, despite everything she's gone through, she still believes in true love.

But then she meets Damian.

When Alexis shows up into his life, Damian's caught by surprise. She's different. She's sweet, innocent, and feisty. But above all, this woman didn't respond to his charm and piercing-blue eyes the way every other woman did. To Damian, she's his ultimate challenge.

Could Alexis be the girl that will break through Damian's wall of perpetual bachelorhood without getting hurt? Or will Damian remain true his ways and break Alexis's heart and her hopes of true love?

## ABOUT THE AUTHOR

Jessica Wood writes new adult contemporary romance.

While she has lived in countless cities throughout the U.S., her heart belongs to San Francisco. To her, there's something seductively romantic about the Golden Gate Bridge, the steep rolling hills of the city streets, the cable cars, and the Victorian-style architecture.

Jessica loves a strong, masculine man with a witty personality. While she is headstrong and stubbornly independent, she can't resist a man who takes control of the relationship, both outside and inside of the bedroom.

She loves to travel internationally, and tries to plan a yearly trip abroad. She also loves to cook and bake, and—to the benefit of her friends—she loves to share. She also enjoys ceramics and being creative with her hands. She has a weakness for good (maybe bad) TV shows; she's up-to-date on over 25 current shows, and no, that wasn't a joke.

And it goes without saying, she loves books—they're like old and dear friends who have always been there to make her laugh and make her cry.

The one thing she wishes she had more of, is time.

If you would like to follow or contact Jessica Wood, you can do so through the following:

**Mailing List**: http://jessicawoodauthor.com/mailing-list/

**Blog**: http://jessicawoodauthor.com

**Facebook**: www.facebook.com/jessicawoodauthor

**Twitter**: http://twitter.com/jesswoodauthor

**Pinterest**: http://pinterest.com/jessicawooda/

Printed in Great Britain
by Amazon